The City

of the

Fireflies

The Glimmer Saga: Book 2

D E McCluskey

D E McCluskey

Copyright © 2022 by D E McCluskey

ISBN 978-1-914381-05-8

Dammaged Production
www.dammaged.com

The City of the Fireflies

For Christopher, Gary, and Liam

Family…

3

D E McCluskey

Part One.

1.

THE SUN WAS shining in the deep azure of the sky, casting its warmth over the lush valley below it. The winter snows had receded, and the hibernating foliage was daring to rear its head, ready for another spring, summer, and autumn. The colours that populated the valley were breath taking. Some hadn't been seen in this vicinity for years. The feeling through the city was this was going to be a glorious year.

Along with the arrival of the colour, there had been a buzz throughout the washhouses and marketplaces of the town, talk of another new arrival. A very important one.

A royal one.

Bunting had been hung from the roofs of the houses, and decorations adorned the windows and doors of shops. The day that King Leopold and Queen Rabia were to expect their first child was rapidly approaching. The hot talk around the grog shops was that it was to be a boy. A strong boy. An heir to the throne, and a justified lineage to the peaceful reign of his father.

All of Carnelia held its breath.

It was true to say that the queen had not had a good pregnancy. There had been a lot of pain and twinges, there had been blood and cramps all the way through to the ninth month. This information had been kept silent from the gossips and loose-lipped drunks of the city; the last thing they wanted was to show any royal weakness to their subjects.

The baby had pushed at the queen's ribs for almost six months, causing pain and limiting her public appearances. She had spent a lot of time in the birthing wing of the hospital.

'The little bugger is so strong, and so eager to get out into the world,' the king would laugh at formal gatherings, while raising a toast of wine to his absent wife. 'He doesn't know what he's doing. It's not his fault.'

Many a midwife would swear testimony that they had heard the queen say, 'I just wish he'd hurry up and get the hell out of there.' This had only been uttered in confidence to either the midwives on hand to help her through her difficulties or the women around her who shared their brief tenures as they were brought in and then out again, babes in arms.

Queen Rabia had been an almost constant patient at the hospital. She had begun to think of herself as a permanent resident. Among the gloom and the pain of her pregnancy, there had, however been one shining light in the birthing wing.

Camarilla.

Camarilla was a lowborn woman who shared an age with Queen Rabia. She also shared her condition. They had been brought into the hospital on the same day, suffering the same agonies; and were both due to give birth to their first-born on the same date.

'It is more than a coincidence, my love,' Queen Rabia told her husband one night when the pain was not so bad and they were alone in their private ward. 'How can it be that in a city as big and as plentiful as ours, we're both brought in on the same night?'

'I hear what you say, my queen, but what of this coincidence?'

'She believes deep in her heart that she is to birth a girl. A girl to be born on the same day as our son. Do you not see the significance?'

The king shook his head. He didn't like this kind of talk. 'Rabia,' he tutted, patting her hand. 'Our son is highborn. He must marry a highborn woman, not a lowborn wench's daughter that you have taken to your fancy.'

The queen shook her head and pulled her husband close. 'She's no wench. She's educated, she can read. She knows the stars. She tells me stories of the old ways, the ways of the Glimm and the purple."

'Fairy tales, my dear, pure and simple fairy tales.' Leopold laughed, pulling away from his wife to get himself comfortable in his chair.

'Well, that's as may be, but she entertains me. She doesn't hold with airs and graces in my presence. I feel like I know her, maybe *have* known her in a past life. I believe our paths have crossed for a reason.'

'Folly,' he laughed, patting his hand on his wife's bloated belly. 'But if it amuses you, I'll play along with it. Keep her in your circle if you must, but I pray you to heed my words. Our children will not wed.'

~~~~

The birth came, and it was a difficult one, almost as difficult as the pregnancy had been. The queen was attended by six midwives for the full eighteen hours of her non-stop, gruelling labour. Complication after complication was conquered, and sure enough, eventually the Kingdom of Carnelia had its heir. A son was born to Leopold and Rabia. His name would be on the lips of everyone's by the next morning.

'All hail Prince Thaddius!'

He was a strong and healthy child. He had the truest and thickest royal blood running through his veins. King Leopold could not have been more pleased.

The queen, however, was in a poor condition. She had lost a lot of blood during childbirth, and the hopes of her survival were slimming by the day. Leopold would not accept this. He demanded to know what was happening, and why. He blustered his way through the hospital until he reached the master in charge of the midwives. He was a small man who had taken to wearing a black robe. He wore lenses on his eyes; these, he claimed, helped him to see clearer.

'What is being done regarding my wife?' Leopold demanded after he had thrust his way into the master's chambers.

The small man stood upon his entering; his hooded head bowed low. 'I'm afraid, Your Majesty, there is very little we can do. The difficult birth, coupled with the painful pregnancy have been too much for the queen's blood. She has lost too much of the liquid of life, and what little she has left has poisoned itself in the womb extraction.'

'This is simply not good enough,' Leopold bellowed. 'I want something done, and I want it done now.'

The master quaked at the king's wrath. He cowered, clenching and unclenching his fingers. 'There is one procedure that we can do,' he stuttered. 'It involves finding a biological match for her blood and transfusing it, completely. This will, of course, be fatal to the donor.'

'I don't care about the donor; I can't bring up a baby on my own. Find the match. Tell them that if they were to do this deed, then their family will be well protected by the seal of the Kingdom of Carnelia. They will want for nothing. I will see that they have lands and titles—'

'Sire,' the master interrupted. 'We have already found a match.'

The king looked at the doctor. His face flashed angry for a moment at the audacity of the man interrupting him mid flow, but then he pondered on what he had just been told. 'You already have a match?' he repeated. 'Well, who is it, man? Name them and I'll speak to them personally.'

'It is a lady, sire. A lady who has been a constant companion to your wife, right through their pregnancies. Her name is — '

'Camarilla.' It was the king's turn to interrupt.

The doctor bowed his head in reverence of the woman's name. She had been a model patient, but now he knew he had condemned her to death. Power and privilege would win over the lowborn every time. 'You know of her?'

'Yes. My wife has spoken of her, often. They have formed a bond of friendship.'

'They are rather close, my lord. She is the only one, of our knowledge, within this Kingdom to have the same blood type. We may be able to find another, but your wife's time draws closer. She'd surely not survive the search.'

The King's face was solemn, but his eyes told a different story. It was a glimpse of light at the end of a long, dark tunnel. This *had* to happen. He knew he could not, and would not, bring up a child alone. He was the king, there were important things for him to do. There were many wild boars in the woods that needed to be hunted. 'I will speak with her. Where is she?'

The doctor sighed. 'She's in the labour ward; she recently gave birth. It was a healthy baby girl. Both mother and child are fine.'

'Is she good for visitors?'

The doctor bowed his head again. 'Yes, my lord. I'm sure she would welcome such a … stately visitor.'

'Good,' the King replied. 'Her child is about to receive everything she never had.'

2.

THE KING ENTERED the birthing wing like a hurricane whipping a frenzy through the countryside. The lights were low and sombre due to the late hour. A few midwives were treating women in beds dotted around the room, soothing heads, and emptying chamber pots. The Royal Guard entered before him, ordering everyone to halt what they were doing and prepare themselves for the royal entrance.

The doctor on duty blustered from his small office at the back of the ward. His white coat was covered in stains that could have been dried blood, and he fiddled with his buttons as he addressed the king. 'Sire, what do we owe the honour of your visit? Your wife is in the dependency unit. If you would permit me to say, these ladies need their rest. The excitement of a guest of your stature would—'

'I'm here to see one called Camarilla. Would you direct me to her?'

The doctor pushed his hair away from his face and licked his lips. 'Yes of course, my liege.' He bowed low as he led the king towards the bed at the end of the long room.

The smell was an uncomfortable mixture of blood, sweat, and disinfectant, and the king didn't want to venture too far in, practicality however, stated the woman could not come to him. 'I'll need privacy for what we are about to discuss. Please draw curtains around us and leave.'

The doctor did as he was bidden, although reluctantly. He knew the nature of the king's business and ordered the nurses to locate a privacy screen.

Once the king was satisfied, and the doctor was gone, he awoke Camarilla with a rough shake. 'Camarilla. Camarilla, do you know who I am?' he asked in a hushed voice.

The woman on the bed roused. She looked up at him. He saw she was still one third asleep, one third in awe, and the other third in agony, but was satisfied when her eyes widened as they recognised who he was.

'Your Majesty,' she mumbled, rubbing her hands over her face, attempting to sit up. The agony of her manoeuvre was not lost on him, and he attempted to help by patting her pillows, uselessly.

'Then you know why I'm here. I will assume you have been made aware of the service I ask of you.'

The woman on the bed nodded, her lips trembled as she did.

'It is something that involves great sacrifice on your part. But know this, it is a sacrifice that will not go without reward.' Leopold knew when a lowborn was asked a favour for a king or a queen, they were honour bound not to refuse. They knew it would not be in their favour to deny the request.

Camarilla was now wide awake.

'I promise, by my crown and sceptre, your daughter will be raised as if she were my very own. She will want for nothing. Think about your child having the title of Lady. She will own lands and fine jewels. She will marry into nobility.'

His voice softened as he leaned in to the terrified woman on the bed, but it was cold and demanding. She could smell mint plant on his breath as he leaned in close. 'What can you offer her, Camarilla? I've checked, I know that you work in a baker's kitchen. You start work at three in the morning and don't finish until six in the evening. What sort of opportunities can you offer this child?' He sat up away from the wretch on the bed, his face a mask of disgust. 'Do you even *know* who the father is?'

Camarilla shook her head slowly. She was too scared for her daughter, and herself to answer aloud.

'No? See, I didn't think so. Your child is a female bastard. She is already at a disadvantage. She will be whoring herself in the taverns by age thirteen, pregnant by fifteen, and possibly dead by thirty. Is that what you want for her?'

Camarilla shook her head again.

'Agree to my terms and she will want for nothing.'

Thick tears welled in her eyes as she eyed the infant in the cot next to her bed. 'How will my child get her nourishment if not from me?' she whispered, not able to muster anything stronger.

'She will be getting nourishment from you.'

Camarilla cocked her head. It was only a small movement, but it told him everything he needed to know. This woman was open to his offer. 'Rabia, your queen, my wife, has just given birth to a son. Her body is producing milk akin to yours. Once your blood courses through her veins, she will suckle your child.'

'I have your promise on this?' she asked, her confidence growing now.

'You have my solemn word, as your king.'

The woman looked to her child for a moment longer. She longed to kiss the child's head, a lingering caress, but the pain and discomfort prevented her from doing so. She closed her eyes. 'Then, for the good of my child, and for the good of my queen. I'll do as you ask.'

There was little doubt in the matter, Leopold thought as his cold eyes regarded the wretch on the bed. He patted her arm in a half-hearted attempt to reassure her. 'I'll start the process right away. We have very little time. Your friend, the queen, grows weaker by the hour. It pains me to see her like that.'

'Sire ...?' Camarilla asked, as Leopold rose from his chair.

'Yes, my child?' he replied, rolling his eyes. He was in a hurry to get away from this filthy place and go home to take to a bath.

Camarilla swallowed and breathed a shallow sigh. 'I need you to promise me one thing, then I will sign my blood, and my child over to you.'

'Name it,' he replied, already bored with this conversation.

'Her name ...' Camarilla began.

'Do not worry, child. She'll receive a royal name, a name befitting a Lady.'

'She already has a name that is befitting to a lady, sire.' Camarilla closed her eyes as more tears streaked down her cheeks. 'Her name is ... Endellion.'

3.

KING LEOPOLD WAS true to his word. That very night he had his lawmen draw up a contract between himself and the estate of Camarilla. The contract stated that the child's name would stay as Endellion, that she would live within the castle walls, she would be given the title of Lady, and she would be given a generous monthly allowance. In short, she would want for nothing. Even her education would be linked directly with that of Prince Thaddius.

As part of the contract, the king and queen would see to it that Lady Endellion would marry into nobility and that she would receive one hundred percent of her very own dowry. All this was done, simply with the signing of the legal document.

For Endellion to receive a better life than she could have ever given her, Camarilla had to give consent for the Carnelian doctors to drain all the blood from her body and use it for a complete transfusion with Queen

Rabia. This would obviously result in her death, but she could rest easy in the knowledge that Endellion would be well cared for.

After consultation with a lawyer knowledgeable in such contracts, provided by King Leopold, the contract was duly signed. The signature was witnessed by the lawyer, the doctor on duty, and a nurse who was on duty that night.

The transfusion was scheduled for the very next day.

'Will I be allowed to spend my last night holding my child?' Camarilla asked the lawmaker, holding the baby as if her very life depended on the contact, which of course, it did.

'Yes, you can,' he replied. 'But you will be under constant supervision by the royal guard, in case you attempt to renege on the deal.'

Camarilla's face was nestling in the wispy hair of her child. She was taking in as much baby smell as she could, hoping it would give her the courage to do what was necessary. 'I won't, sir. I want what's best for my Endellion. I'll not be able to provide for her, and she needs, no, she deserves, the very best in life.'

'Right, my work here is done.' The lawmaker stood and held Camarilla's arm for a moment. 'You are doing the right thing; you do know that, don't you? For your daughter and for the Kingdom of Carnelia.' The tall, thin man smiled down upon her before turning and striding out of the room. He stopped when he got to the door. As his thin fingers grasped the handle, attempting to turn it, he sighed. He turned and looked at the doctor and the nurses present. Finally, his solemn gaze fell upon the pathetic figure of Camarilla, still grasping her wriggling babe to her breast. He blinked slowly before swallowing. 'The queen ...' he began, then paused and dropped his eyes, purposely averting them from everyone in the room, '... is to know nothing of this transaction.'

'Of course, sir,' the doctor replied. 'We'll administer potions that will make her sleep for hours before and after the procedure. All she'll know is that she is growing stronger and that poor Camarilla died due to complications at the birth.'

'Then the king will suggest she brings the child into court and help with her upbringing. The queen will be happy in her ignorance of the situation,' the lawman concluded. He then bade them a good day without once making eye contact. He left the room quickly, without another word.

4.

CAMARILLA SPENT THE night in fevered prayer to The Great Lord Glimm. She asked nothing of him but to look over her child, to raise her wanting for nothing, and for the king to keep his word. Each time she gazed on the small child suckling at her breast, tears welled in her eyes. They were not tears for her and her impending doom but for her not being able to watch her child grow and prosper.

'Goodbye, my sweet Endellion,' she whispered repeatedly through the night to the child. 'I would have loved to have known you. But I have done you a service, my sweet. You are destined for great things; things I could never have given you. Always be aware, Endellion. Look out for yourself and for those you love, and remember child, small acorns can bring down mountains.'

Eventually, fatigue overcame her, and Camarilla slept with the child still suckling at her breast. When she was in a deep sleep, the nurses removed Endellion and placed her into a private room. They injected

Camarilla with milk from the flowers that grew wild in the hills, and poor woman's slumber deepened.

Under cover of the night, a comatose Queen Rabia was wheeled into the same private room. Tubes that had been cleansed with alcohol were prepared, along with sharp, hollow needles.

One of the needles was pushed into the queen's left arm. A foot pump was activated, and the tube began to fill with her viscous, poisoned blood.

The doctor paused as he looked at the healthy sleeping woman on the bed before him. In his hand, he held another sharp needle, the needle that would bring the death of the innocent woman before him. His hands were shaking, and moist. He looked around the room at the expectant faces, each staring intently at him. He felt the weight of their stares keenly, but one stare especially.

King Leopold's.

The king had demanded to be present, and no one had the courage to attempt to dissuade him. He sat at the top of the bed, stroking his wife's hair and looking at the doctor. 'Well?' he said, cocking his head. The word was spoken softly, but the malice within it was ripe.

The doctor blinked at the word, as if snapping back into the room from a dream. He indicated to a nurse to cut the woman's arm and the queen's other arm. She did this without hesitation, covering the two incisions with swabs.

The doctor inserted the needle with the tube attached to it into the arm of the woman and activated the foot pump. Thick blood filled the tube. There was no disparity in colour or viscosity, the only difference between this blood and the queen's was this one was healthy. This blood had no right to be leaving its host. The other end of the tube was inserted into the fresh incision in the queen's arm.

The process of the blood transfusion had begun.

The king watched as the tube entered his wife's arm. He leaned in close as the dark fluid began to flow, heading towards its new home. A ghost of a smile broke on his face as he watched Rabia's face drain of colour before turning purple. There was a moment of panic as her lips began to turn the dark blue of death. It was followed by a hushed sigh of relief from everyone, especially the doctor, as tendrils of white, then pink, then red began to bloom in her cheeks.

Leopold's attention turned towards the lowborn wretch. His smile grew as he watched her face lose its colour and the purple mask deepen. He stepped back a little as she became agitated and began to thrash. The doctor, hoping to keep order, and to keep the flow of blood even, ordered the nurses to hold her down.

The king's brow ruffled as he looked at the doctor.

'It's a natural reaction,' he soothed. 'The body doesn't want to die, no matter how heavily sedated she is. She will instinctively fight the process of death.'

'Well, it's distressing. Can't we just cut her throat now and have it done with?' he asked, turning his attentions back to his wife.

'No, Sire,' the doctor replied, his eyes tinged with confusion. 'We need every drop oxygenated. If it's too distressing for you, then may I invite you to leave the room and we'll call you when it's done?'

'Doctor, I will remind you who you are addressing. I would hold your tongue, or I'll have it removed. I'm sure you can perform medicine without one, eh?' Leopold replied without looking at him.

The doctor nodded and closed his mouth.

As Camarilla's thrashing subsided, the nurse released her grip and slowly, reverently, stepped away from the table. The only sound in the room now was the twitching of Camarilla's arms and legs against the blankets. Everyone present, including the king, held their breath.

After a short while, the doctor stepped forward and touched two fingers against Camarilla's neck. He closed his eyes and exhaled. 'It's done,' he whispered. 'The process is complete. Camarilla is deceased. May the Lords of Glimm take her.'

'Excellent,' King Leopold announced loudly as he stood from his seat at the top of the bed. 'I'll now retire to my chambers. It's been a long and arduous night. Please, wake me when the queen rouses.'

'Of course, Your Highness,' the doctor replied as he watched the king leave, followed closely by his royal guard. When the door closed, he closed his eyes and whispered beneath his breath, 'May the Lords of Glimm forgive you for what you have done this night.' He regarded the two bodies on the beds. One was glowing with health and sleeping; the other was purple and emaciated in death. He shivered as he pulled the blanket over Camarilla's face. He then turned towards the queen and put his fingers on her neck. In complete contrast to her friend's, her skin was warm and her heartbeat was healthy and strong.

He ordered the nurses to remove Queen Rabia to a recovery room.

When he was alone, he prayed over the body of Camarilla.

5.

THE SUN SHONE through the curtains, creating a shaft of light in the darkness of the room. The shaft was alive with a hundred million dust motes dancing and swooping within. The hushed tones of someone doing their best to be silent roused Queen Rabia from her slumber. She opened her eyes and waited for her vision to become unclouded. When it did, she found herself in unfamiliar surroundings. The chambermaid who had awoken her was standing at the end of her bed, the single shaft of light falling favourably on her profile, and the queen recognised her pretty face as soon as she smiled.

'Where am I?' she asked. Her throat hurt as she spoke.

'You're safe, Your Highness,' the chambermaid replied. 'There's someone here to see you.'

As the girl walked away, she gestured towards the door, where a silhouette stood in the shadows. She recognised the outline straight away.

'I had you moved, my wife,' Leopold whispered. 'I couldn't stand the thought of you waking in that hospital.'

'My child?' she winced as she attempted to sit up. Her arms instinctively reaching to her belly, where her baby had sat for so long. She looked around the room, her eyes not focusing on anything, or anyone as they wildly swept from object to object, face to face. Her own face transformed from a mask of wild confusion to one of agony as bolts of pain shot up both arms. 'Where's my child?' she sobbed, ignoring the pain. 'Did my child survive the birth?'

The king had made his way into the room and began to stroke her hair, whispering, soothing her of her terror. 'Yes, my love, yes. Please, calm yourself. Our child is strong and healthy, like any prince would be.'

On hearing her husband's words, Rabia's face calmed. Her brow flattened and her tensed shoulders visibly relaxed. She lay back into the bed, melting into the pillows. An exhausted smile cracked her dry lips. 'A boy then?' she asked. Her voice was hoarse and laboured but also relieved. 'A strong boy?'

Leopold stood and hooked his thumbs through the leather belt of his trousers. 'Yes, my love,' he announced, more to the room than to his wife. The smile on his face in danger of snapping his face in two. 'The strongest boy ever to be born into the service of Carnelia.'

'It is a time for celebration then,' the queen said, attempting to raise from her bed once again. The pain was evident in her creased features. 'Have you ordered the bunting to be raised?'

Leopold watched her trying to get up and laid his hands on her shoulders, lightly coercing her to stay in the bed. 'Not yet. You've been most unwell, my queen. There were … complications.'

'Complications?' she asked as she allowed her husband to persuade her back down. 'What complications?'

'It is nothing for you to fret about. Everything is fine. You have fully recovered, and that is all that matters.' He gestured to one of the maids, who hurriedly left the room, returning a few seconds later with a bundle of swaddling clothes. The bundle was crying and wriggling. 'Here's the little man now,' he boasted, accepting the bundle from the maid. 'May I introduce you to Prince Thaddius, our son.'

Rabia's face lightened at her husband's announcement. The young woman she had once been shone through her eyes as she pushed back the mask of her agonising pregnancy and tough labour. 'My father's name,' she gushed. A small bout of coughing overtook her, and she held her bruised arms to her belly again.

Leopold's eyes shifted nervously to the doctor next to him, but the doctor offered him a shake of his head and, more importantly, a smile.

She held out her arms, accepting the package offered to her, thankfully.

'I thought it a fitting name for a prince, and for a king-to-be. It is my belief the kingdom will be in safe hands with this one.'

~~~~

King Leopold beamed as his wife accepted the child from his grasp. A tear welled in his eye, and he wiped it before anyone in the room could see. But it was too late, and news of the king crying at the birth of his son became the talk of the grog houses that night, and the next few nights to come.

As he watched his wife hold their child, a cloud passed over his features. *I am not an animal,* he thought, attempting to dismiss the deeds he had done to protect his wife and child. *I did what I had to do. What any father would do for his wife and child. I did for the whole of Carnelia!*

However, deep in his heart, he knew the truth. He had done it for himself. He knew he would soon bore of the labours of a child, and he would need Rabia to raise the future king.

Under instruction from a handmaiden, the queen bared a breast for the infant to feed; as she did, a noise from the other room caught everyone's attention. It was a loud, high-pitched cry. Very much a child's cry. She looked up at her husband.

'Leopold, what's that noise? Pray, did I have twins?' she asked.

Leopold grinned again. *Here it is,* he thought as he looked towards the sound of crying in the other room. 'No, Rabia, you didn't have twins,' her soothed her, laying his hands on her head again. 'But you will need to brace yourself, my love. I have some news, ill news.' He bit the inside of his cheek before continuing. 'Your friend Camarilla,' he began. 'She did not survive the birthing. Complication after complication took her away to be with her Gods. They did, however, show mercy on her child, a baby girl. I took the liberty of naming her Endellion …'

Another handmaiden appeared at his side, carrying another bundle of crying swaddling clothes.

'Oh my, my poor Camarilla. She was such good counsel to me.' A tear dripped down the queen's face. 'Hand me the child. She will be raised as our own. We can tell the world I had twins …'

'That will not be so easy, my love,' Leopold smiled. He was nervous, but he didn't want to show his weakness to those in the room. 'There were many doctors and nurses attending the birth. Word is already out that you had but one child, a boy. It would cause scandal and uncertainty if we were to announce suddenly, we had twins. No, we cannot raise her as our own. But I made a solemn promise, on her mother's deathbed; I gave my word that her child would not need, nor want, for anything.'

'We'll bring her up a Lady then?'

'Aye,' Leopold replied, nodding with his eyes closed. He couldn't look at his wife just then. 'We'll bring her up a Lady.'

The second child, Endellion, had already attached herself to Rabia's other breast and was happily suckling away.

~~~~

When everyone had left and the rooms had been scrubbed and cleaned, the doctor sat alone with his thoughts. On a gurney next to him

28

was the corpse of Camarilla. He had been given the duty of disposing of the body, along with any evidence of the wrongdoing on the king's behalf.

Earlier that day, he had overseen the digging of a pauper's grave some three miles outside of the castle walls. It was shallow, and in rough earth. King Leopold had ordered no markings for the grave, but the doctor was a religious man. He had fashioned from wood a makeshift ball and painted it red. He placed it in the hands of the corpse next to him and summoned the men who would take the unfortunate wretch to her final resting place.

'May the Great Lord Glimm himself forgive me, and us, for what we have done,' he whispered with his head held low as the men pushed the gurney out of the hospital.

D E McCluskey

Part Two

1.

ALMOST A YEAR had passed since Carnelia had fallen at the hands of Endellion—masquerading as Queen Cassandra—and annexed to the Kingdom of Azuria. Most of that time had been taken locating, removing, and either burying or cremating the victims of the black rain that had fallen on that fateful day.

There had been mutterings in the streets, the homes of the survivors, and the grog shops regarding the events that had led to the fall of kingdom. Whispered talk of dark magic and cursed rain, of spells that had been cast on the citizens, causing them to turn murderous, to tear each other apart like savages in the streets.

Each survivor had their own beliefs, stories, and conspiracies to spread regarding that fateful day, and they had no problem, once the beer and wine had been flowing, letting others know what they thought. They had to be careful, of course, no one could know the allegiances of the person they were talking to. One slipped tongue or loose lip could get a person in trouble—the kind of trouble where they, and what remained of their families, were never seen again.

The ease that the Azurian devils had sacked their kingdom fuelled this gossip, and now that life was changing within the kingdom's walls, unease was felt everywhere. Where once there had been peace and harmony, an atmosphere of violence and ill-will prevailed. An Azurian screw was turning, affecting the lives of every survivor. It was more than apparent that life within the kingdom, formerly known as Carnelia, was not what it had once been, nor might it ever be.

2.

'ALEXANDER. ALEX, WHERE are you? We must leave at once.' The voice travelled up the stairs from their living chambers, into his chambers. 'Alexander, you must be ready. We have to leave go right now.'

Alexander wrapped his head beneath his pillow, attempting to block the shill voice of his sister. 'I'm coming, Cass,' he shouted. 'You don't need to scream at me so loud,' he added, quiet enough so only he could hear it. He unwrapped the pillow from his head and threw it across the room. Lying on his back, the tall, soon-to-be-twelve-year-old, exhaled a deep sigh. 'Why do the days always have to start so early?' he spat as he prised his body from the comfort of his bed. His motivation was helped along by the smells of fresh bread and bacon being prepared from somewhere outside his room. He picked up the clothing that was neatly folded at the end of his bed and began to dress. 'What do you need me for?' he shouted down the stairs.

'Because, my brother and knight, I need the most loyal and bravest of men at my sides at all times. I leave for what used to be Carnelia, post-haste. There has been sightings of Rebels, and Ferals, on the roads between here and there.'

'So, take your guard. I can barely hold a broadsword yet, or swing a mace ...' he replied in bored tones.

'It is not about swords and maces, brother. It's about who you trust and how close you keep your own,' the disembodied voice replied.

'If the Carnelians are all dead, then who, or what, are Ferals?' he asked, wrapping his cloak over his shoulders.

'A group of ungrateful, undisciplined, unworthy types who oppose our occupation of Carnelia,' his sister replied, her voice sounding closer.

He looked towards the doorway and was surprised to see her standing there, dressed in jodhpurs and boots, her long, dark hair tied back by a strap of leather, ready for a day's riding.

'They're too scared to come out and fight us directly. Instead, they try to intimidate us with terrorist acts.'

'Can't we just send the fireflies after them?' he asked, buckling his cloak around his neck.

'If only we could. They are proving hard to find, besides, I think there's something strange about them, something that the fireflies don't like too much, and I don't blame them.' She laughed. 'I don't like them either.'

Although he didn't quite get the joke, he smiled as he presented himself to the woman he thought of as his sister but was really a witch in disguise.

'Come on. You look fine.'

'Why do we need to go to Carnelia? You're the queen, I'm the prince, surely there's someone else who can do the work that's required there,' he asked as they made their way towards the kitchens.

'I'm the sovereign, as are you. These people are lost, and scared. They need to know I have their best interests at heart. No more questions now, brother. We must eat before we ride if we're to meet our first outpost by nightfall.'

With that, they entered the kitchens. The fantastic aromas hit his nose, taking his mind away from the lingering questions he still pondered.

Huge plates had been prepared for them, stacked with seared meats and freshly baked bread.

After they had eaten their fill and packed bags with leftovers for later, they mounted their steeds and, along with one hundred and fifty men and an unseen swarm of fireflies, they headed off to Carnelia.

3.

IN A CAMP, deep in the woods, off the main thoroughfare between the two kingdoms, the real Queen Cassandra had earned an uneasy trust, and a bearable respect from the Ferals with whom she rode alongside. It was an alliance that had been uneasily sought at first, but she had eventually proven herself to be an asset to their group. She had been the enemy as the Queen of Azuria; but as word passed that there was another woman with the likeness of Queen Cassandra of Azuria—this one riding into Carnelia and out again carrying victory banners—the Ferals had reluctantly believed her story and taken her into their trust.

The Rebel's leader, Robert Ambric, had endorsed her by confirming with the two groups that it was indeed a witch they were dealing with. A witch who had taken the guise of Cassandra and singlehandedly roused the Azurians into battle. A battle that Ambric believes they won by ill means. On the say of Ambric, Cassandra had been welcomed into the fold of the Ferals and enlisted within the second group, currently encamped within striking distance of one of the Azurian strongholds.

Tonight, Cassandra had taken the second watch. It was her favourite. It gave her opportunity to study her Glimmer, away from the prying eyes of the rest of the camp.

The blue orb that her brother had gifted her on the day she left Azuria for the last time, a morning that seemed like centuries ago, was finally opening its mysteries to her. She had found, more by accident than design, that the orb has powers, powers that had helped her on more than one occasion. Each time she used it, she communicated with a strange order of men, the Glimm. They had taught her how to control the orb, how to channel the powers instilled within it. They informed her that their race had long ago mastered the elements of nature, animals, even people. Their magic ran the gauntlet of both light and dark, and as custodian of this Glimmer, she now had access to the sum of their ancient knowledge.

It was a very powerful gift.

Although she was still a long way from fully understanding how it worked, she was learning and growing stronger. Many times, she would remove herself to unseen parts, places where no roaming eyes could see what she was doing, and practise. The Glimm informed her that she needed all the practise she could get to master the powers. They had also informed her of a second Glimmer, one equally as powerful as the one she owned. They warned that if one solitary person should become custodian of both Glimmers, that person would become all powerful; and with great power comes great responsibility.

Tonight, was a particularly dark night. The clouds were thick above them, and the area they had chosen for camp was dense with trees. She had slept all she needed during the first watch and performed her own watch admirably, but more sleep was not in her plans when her duty concluded. Once she'd been relieved, she took herself into the woods, her hand buried deep inside her pocket, protecting her glowing treasure.

She recalled how it had saved her life on many occasions.

Without understanding what she had done, she had commanded a stoat to bring her food while imprisoned in her high dungeon. It had heeded her commands, and she had survived that ordeal. She hungered to replicate whatever command she had given that animal. She had an idea that the understanding of these powers would be key to ending the unholy occupation of Carnelia by her own kingdom.

She needed something she could control, something to combat the ghastly fireflies Endellion had commanded when she attacked and imprisoned her.

There had been some success in this endeavour. However, it had been limited and very frustrating.

So, she found herself a comfortable nook far enough away from the camp for privacy, but close enough for her to know she was safe. She sat in the heather with her back against a sturdy tree and removed the orb from her pocket. She held it, cupped delicately in both hands, and closed her eyes. *Bring me a bird from a tree holding a twig in its mouth*, she commanded in her head.

She opened her eyes expectantly, but nothing happened.

Undeterred, she closed her eyes again. *Bring forth a fox carrying ripe hazelnuts.*

Still, nothing happened.

She tried again with a rabbit, a mole, a pack of rats … all to no avail.

Unconvinced that she was ever going to understand the orb, control the power she had personally witnessed and, at fleeting times, held, she considered summoning the Glimm to ask them why. But she knew if she did, the cryptic answers they gave would confuse her even more, and she'd end up spending the day deciphering them.

Getting up from the floor, she pocketed the orb and made her way back to camp. There would be no more practise today.

As she got close, she could hear chaos and confusion coming from where the tents had been raised. There were men running, shouting and screaming at each other. Flaming torches were being passed around and swooped to the ground. She could see silhouettes of panicked men sprinting from tent to tent.

It's an attack, she thought and crouched low into the bushes.

She had the element of surprise and hoped to use it to her advantage. As she crept closer, she squinted, trying to make sense of the scene before her. There were no noises she associated with battle. No clanging of steel or screams of dying men. There was nothing of the blue armour of Azuria to be seen anywhere. She crept closer still, hoping to get a better understanding of what was happening, unsheathing her sword, ready for her own attack.

What she saw as she got closer made her laugh out loud, and she re-sheathed her weapon, shaking her head.

Amid the flashing of torches and the shouting men, she could see the camp was encumbered with wild animals, all of them making nuisances of themselves. A large bird with a long twig in its mouth was swooping at the petrified men below. The poor creature looked like it was trying to give the twig to someone, but every time it got close, all it got for its endeavours was a swipe with a fiery torch. A large fox was chasing rabbits around the tents, and several molehills had been created in the clearing. There was also a pack of rats hiding in the twilight glow of the coming day, skulking back and forth.

Cassandra laughed, clasping her hands over her face. 'I did it,' she gasped. 'It worked, after all.'

One of the guards became alerted to her presence in the bushes.

'What are you laughing at?' he asked, waving his torch around as if it were a sword, trying to fend off the rats. 'Get over here and help. The camp is overrun with, with vermin.'

'Nonsense,' Cass replied and reached into her pocket to touch the Glimmer. *Release them from my thrall*, she thought, her eyes closed.

All at once, the animals scarpered away into the woods from whence they came.

'Thank the Lord for that,' the guard shouted as the camp became peaceful again.

Yes, Cass thought with a grin. *Thank the Great Lord Glimm.*

4.

ENDELLION AND HER entourage reached the first encampment on the third day of their long journey towards Azuria. It was referred to as an encampment, but it was really a fortress; large and well defended. Its grey walls were built from blocks of jagged rocks, built to repel invaders. The camp was built to hold at least three hundred men, and a strong contingent of then were Azurian guards. There were cooking facilities and baths within the walls, everything that a travelling queen needed to rest after a long ride.

The advanced royal guard had ridden ahead to alert the camp of the arrival of the queen, and all preparations had been made for her appearance.

'I must meditate, Alexander. I will leave you in charge here,' Endellion, still in her Cassandra guise, told her younger brother once they were safely within the confines of their private quarters. 'Order the men to eat the meat and drink some wine, but not too much, we leave at first light.'

'Yes, my queen.' Alexander bowed, enjoying the idea of overseeing the fortress.

'Oh, order them to get baths too. Some of them stink worse than the horses,' she added, closing the door between them, leaving him in the room alone.

He grinned as he looked around, then exited with his head held high.

Once inside her sparsely furnished chamber, away from nosey courtesans, she locked the heavy wooden door and leaned her back against it. Reaching into the secret pocket in her riding garb, she greedily grasped the metallic ball hidden within.

'Glimm, release me from this form. Bring Endellion back,' she whispered.

A wind blew around the room, or more precisely, around the young woman in the room. It whirled, whipping at her dark hair. Her facial features began to change, slowly. Her skin aged, and the darkness of her hair flowed away like milk from a bottle. The youthful shine of black dulled and brittle slivers of silver appeared. The young Cassandra was gone, and the once beautiful Endellion appeared in her place. She released a long, slow sigh and her shoulders relaxed, as if the transformation had taken considerable effort.

She sat, cross legged on the floor, and removed the Glimmer from the folds of her tunic and held it in both hands.

With her eyes closed, she whispered. 'Come to me. Now.'

Instantly, she was transported from the chambers and into the dark, musty throne room. The room was bare, except for an old altar with two skeletons fused to the top of it. It smelled of aged stone, dust, foliage, and death.

She enjoyed being here.

'What is thy bidding?' a voice asked.

She turned and was not surprised to see a man standing behind her. He was short, with long white hair that flowed into his white beard. He was one of the Brotherhood of the Glimm. There was an X-shaped scar carved between his large bushy eyebrows, deep into the aged skin of his face.

'I command you to tell me more of the Throne of Glimm. Where is it in the real world?' she commanded.

The man looked at her. The soft, understanding expression he had on his face did not change. He spread his arms and gestured around him. 'You are here,' he replied.

'In the real word,' she snapped.

The man's expression still did not alter. 'I have told you, Endellion. This is the real world. I have also told you that if you seek to physically enter the Throne of Glimm, then you must locate the purple.'

'What does that even mean?' she shouted, her mouth tightening into a white line. 'Why do you give me cryptic answers?'

'The question was cryptic; therefore, the answer must be too.'

'How can my question be cryptic?' she shouted again, curling her fists into tight balls, all the better to strike something with. 'I asked was where it is!'

'And I told you. To enter the temple, you must locate the purple.'

'Be gone,' she screamed, and instantly she was back in the queen's chambers. She around, her fingers still clawed, desperate for something to smash. However, she knew if she began to tear the place apart, she would illicit the attention of the royal guard, and then she would have to explain who she was and why she was in the queen's chambers.

She took hold of the glimmer and commanded a passing bird to dive bomb the window outside her room, which it promptly did, snapping its neck in the course of its duty. Grinning at her petty cruelty, she put her ear to the door and listened to the men investigating the smashed window. She then took a moment to slip out of the door, unnoticed, into the encampment.

She posed as a scullery maid and passed through the grounds until she came to a service door. With one look around, she opened it and exited into the surrounding forest.

'Fireflies ... to me,' she commanded, once she was deep enough into the heavy trees. A buzz filled the air. It began to throb in her ears. Anyone else would have held their hands to their heads, trying to stop the pulsating thrum from damaging their brains, but not her. She revelled in the noise. A swarm of impossibly large insects appeared over the trees. Each of their yellow and black curved bodies ended in a vicious sting.

Endellion's fireflies hovered overhead, their bodies glowing with menace.

'My children, I need you to be my vanguard. I need you to travel to Carnelia and secure the area of any Rebels or Ferals that may be lying in wait for us. If you encounter anyone from here to there, kill them, regardless of their colours. I cannot allow anything to come between us and securing the Kingdom of Carnelia. Go now,' she commanded.

The fireflies rose into the air, their wings beating rapidly but gracefully as they lifted above the trees and away in unison, in the direction of Carnelia.

She watched them go, smiling as they disappeared into the night.

5.

ROBERT AMBRIC, THE former Carnelian knight, had now become the scourge of Azuria. Followed dutifully by his group, calling themselves The Rebels, made up of the guards who followed him out of Carnelia on that fateful day, had caused havoc with the guard of the watch on what used to be the Carnelian wall. They had chosen to employ a terrorist campaign against the occupation, striking many small but scathing victories to the heart of the occupation. The newly established Azurian guard had been bewildered at how they had been able to foil them at almost every turn, getting inside the castle at will and causing such trouble.

There had been multiple instances of fires within the castle boundaries. Many top officials had been poisoned within their own chambers. At least three dozen horses had inexplicably gone lame within the stables. These were only a few of the methods that The Rebels had claimed as their actions, and the guards were still at a loss as to where, or when, they would strike next. They had not been able to arrest, or to even identify anyone connected with the group or their outlying band, The Ferals.

There were maybe two hundred and fifty soldiers making up the group. In addition to the soldiers, there was something in the region of three hundred civilians who had also followed them out of the kingdom on the day when the black rain had come and turned good people into savages. Ambric was proud of every single one of them. None of them had disobeyed a single order, and everyone had acted, without hesitation, when called upon to do so.

What *had* surprised him was the thousands of civilians who had stayed to continue their lives within the city walls when the fake Queen Cassandra, aided by the Azurian Guard, had arrived to take control of the kingdom. He thought they had done so because they longed to live their lives with the least disruption, and therefore swapped allegiance from Carnelia to Azure. But this did not seem to be the case.

Ambric and his men had been born into this kingdom, they had grown within these walls, they had defended them for years, and knew every nook, every cranny of the city's vulnerabilities. They had not delayed in exploiting this knowledge and had executed many expeditions into the city within the first few months.

There, they had contacted associates within the boundaries and found allies via family and friends still living within the kingdom.

Ambric had found there were many within who shared no love for their new lords, or their new queen.

Many allegiances were made.

These opened opportunities for domestic terrorism. Whenever an opportunity presented itself, it was taken and exploited. This continued until more Azurians began to arrive to help clean up the dead and stake claims on the lands within.

The attacks had become more difficult as the city was becoming heavily populated with repatriated Azurians. The guards on the walls had doubled, sometimes even tripled, and for a while, the attacks had been thwarted. That was when the home allies, the citizens still living within the boundaries, mostly came into play. It was then the poisoning, the laming, and the fires began, causing chaos within the walls.

Ambric and his men began to attack the supply chains to the city, making it as difficult as possible for traders and suppliers to get their goods into the city. No one was safe. Official visitors to the annexed kingdom were easy pickings and were frequently terrorised en-route. Ambric knew that his group were getting the attention of Endellion, the witch, and that was exactly what he wanted.

~~~~

'Sir Ambric, we've received word that Endellion has left the Azurian kingdom threshold,' the advance guardsman reported, out of breath, as he rode his horse into the surroundings of the camp. 'Reports indicate they're travelling with a band of one hundred and fifty royal guards. They arrived at their first outpost late last night.'

'Excellent news.' Ambric smiled as he caught the reins of his horse and tied them to a makeshift corral made of just fallen trees. 'Do we still have Ferals surrounding that outpost?' he asked.

'We do,' the rider responded. As he dismounted the horse, another man came and helped him with his armour. 'There's a small group staking the outpost right now, sir, ready to attack at your say so.'

Ambric shook his head, his long hair, which melted into his shaggy beard, swung wildly as he did. 'No, we don't want them to attack the outpost, that would be suicide. We'll have no more than two days to get this right. Can we get word to the Ferals to stay on the outpost until first light tomorrow morning? This will be an opportunity for us to take Endellion and Outpost Three at the same time. We could cut off the very head of the occupation. Remove the serpent's head, and the body dies with it. We could have Carnelia back with ease.'

'Very well, sir,' the rider replied as he sat at the edge of a campfire and helped himself to some of the meat and drink on offer.

'Dogan,' Ambric said as he strapped a nose bag onto the man's horse.

'Yes, sir?'

'How many times do I have to tell you to drop the *sir*? Since there is no longer a Carnelian realm, I am no longer a knight of that realm. My name is just Robert.'

Dogan looked up at him; a lump of meat in gravy dripped from is chin, back onto the metal plate next to the fire, where it sizzled in the heat. 'I know, sir, but on the day when we freed Carnelia, you will remember me calling you by you name, sir, and you might take offence at it.' He grinned. 'It wouldn't be proper. Old habits die hard, and I would rather not attempt to forge new ones right now, sir.'

Ambric laughed and slapped the man on his shoulder. The force of the slap made him drop more food onto the sizzling metal of the plates by the fire. 'OK then.' He laughed heartily. 'I can't fault your thinking. So, how do we go about getting the word to our allies?'

6.

'PRINCE BERNARD, THERE'S a communication from Sir Ambric and his Rebels. He has knowledge that Endellion, or Cassandra, or whoever it is in charge over there now, has left the city walls with a vanguard. Reports indicate they're heading for Carnelia. They made camp in Outpost Two. Ambric has asked for us to revise our plan for Outpost Three and await his word,' a young man holding a large bird reported to Bernard.

'Excellent news. Can we get word to Feral group two to bring our secret weapon in this morning?' he replied.

The Feral guard smiled. 'Yes, sir, straight away.'

The guard wrote a note and attached it to the leg of the bird he was holding, then let it go. In a fluster of feathers, the bird soared high above the treeline. Bernard watched it fly with a light heart and a smile. He was looking forward to their secret weapon coming into the camp.

'Gremmon, would you call a council of guards for ten minutes? Every Feral we have here in camp will be required for the job in hand,' Bernard asked of the messenger who had just released the bird.

'Yes, Your Highness. Straight away,' he replied, his face changing almost instantly. His eyes sparkled and a smile filled his features, making him look like the young man he was, as opposed to the warrior he was coming to resemble. Ever since Carnelia fell, it had been The Rebels who'd had all the fun. He knew they were real soldiers and his Ferals only trainees, most of them lucky to have been out of the city walls that day, and mostly only because they had been friends with the prince. They had been training hard, learning and relearning how to fight, but up to now, they had only been a nuisance to the enemy, flies to swat away. But secretly, they had been training and planning for an event like this.

As the soldier put word around the camp regarding the council of guards, a healthy buzz erupted to the news. Something was finally happening, something big and worthy of their training.

The meeting tent was full. Every member of the Ferals, except for the perimeter guards, were present, all eager to listen to their prince, excited to hear what the plans could be. All chatter ceased as Bernard walked into the crowded tent.

'Thank you for coming,' he said, loud enough so everyone, even the ones at the back, could hear. 'We've had contact from our friends, The Rebels. They've had word of the movements of the false queen. My friends, all our hard work and patience is about to be put to the test.'

A cheer ripped through the room. Bernard raised his hands to silence them, and they obeyed.

'She'll be at Outpost Three tomorrow night, and that's where we'll spring our trap. There's only one way in and one way out of that fortress, and it will be heavily guarded. But if our attack goes to plan, then it will not be a problem.'

More murmurs of approval filled the room. Bernard looked at their faces. His heart sang as he saw the eagerness in their eyes, the readiness of their bodies. He could smell excitement in the air—to him, it smelt a little like roast pork.

Two hours later, everything was in place. The Ferals would have the outpost surrounded from every angle. They would sit and wait until before first light. There was a change of the guard then. They knew that tired guards were easier to overcome than alert guards. Both sets, the ones coming off shift and the ones coming on, would all be tired, there was always a small window of confusion when they changed hands.

That was the time to strike.

And to strike *softly*.

'Prince Bernard, the secret weapon has arrived. It's coming into camp now,' Gremmon exclaimed as he rushed into the tent from his guard duty. He looked almost fit to burst in his attempts to quell his excitement.

Bernard's heart sang for the second time that night, and the palms of his hands turned moist. He had been looking forward to this for so long, and now it was here. Butterflies raced in his stomach; they were almost too much for him to bear. He tried to hide his excitement from the others, but there was no way of concealing the flush of red in his cheeks. It caused a few whispers, and more than a few laughs. 'Let us go and greet the weapon,' he ordered, making his way out of the tent, into the camp outside.

The vanguard of the second camp of Ferals entered the clearing. The men who had followed Bernard out of the tent began to cheer as more of the second wave filtered in. There was much hugging and slapping of backs. In the months since the fall of Carnelia, Bernard sometimes forgot that his men were old friends and new, made up from all that was left of his Carnelian guard and the academy. He stood and watched with a smile etched firmly on his face as everyone embraced.

He then saw the weapon.

It was a thing to behold.

So deadly, so dangerous, and not to mention … beautiful.

Queen Cassandra of Carnelia walked into the camp. Most of the cheering and back slapping stopped and a reverent hush descended over the gathering. The men in Bernard's camp stood silently, watching her as she passed.

By her demeanour, Bernard knew she was aware of the thoughts regarding her in the camp. She would always be a controversial figure, and he knew that not all the men could bring themselves to truly trust her; even he had issues with it at times. He knew she didn't blame them. Since Endellion had taken her form and ruined their kingdoms in her name, they had only the word of the few people who had witnessed Endellion while she was there, that and the confidence of the most respected person to come from Carnelia, Robert Ambric. Right now, whether the men, or even he, trusted her, she was their best weapon in this fight. If they were to make any impact against Endellion, she may well be their only chance.

'Prince Bernard,' she said, maybe a little too enthusiastically. 'It's pleasing to see you again.' Once it was out of her mouth, it sounded tawdry, and he watched with amusement as her face broke into a crimson blush.

'Queen Cassandra!' he announced. 'I hope our second guard is treating you well.'

She smiled as the blush fell from her face. 'They treat me fine. I've earned their respect, Bernard, and, I hope, yours too.'

You always had it ... he thought, feeling the heat in his own face rise. 'Err, yes.' He coughed. 'The reports I've heard of your progress have been most ... satisfactory.'

This was a small lie, and he knew it, he also knew she knew it too. She smiled, he saw little humour in it, but it wasn't overly harsh either.

'I'll not kill my countrymen, Bernard. I will, however, help take them prisoner, but I cannot kill them.'

'That is commendable. I would have reservations killing my own countrymen too,' he replied, looking around the clearing, trying to find something to distract him from this conversation. *This is too formal*, he thought, *I need to get to her in private.* 'My Lady, would you do me the honour of following me into our meeting tent? We're holding a gathering of the Council of the Guard. It's regarding our attack,' he continued.

'The attack that I'm to be the worm on the hook?' Cassandra asked with a jaunty smile.

Bernard bowed his head, his eyebrows furrowed as he regarded her; his own grin matched hers. 'Yes,' he replied. 'The very one.'

He opened the flap of the tent where they had been having their meeting and held it for her. 'After you,' he said.

She brushed passed him, their arms touching ever so slightly — so slightly, anyone present would have thought it had been an accident; both Cassandra and Bernard knew different.

As they entered, everyone still inside stood.

Once Bernard and Cassandra had taken their seats, everyone followed suit. 'The first order of business I need to address, before we go any further,' Bernard said, his tone light, not as light as his head felt having Cassandra next to him, but light enough, 'is all this *My Prince* rubbish. Carnelia is dead, for the time being anyway. Therefore, as Robert Ambric is no longer a *sir,* I am also no longer a prince. Secondly, as my father died last year in the occupation of Carnelia, technically, I would be king, albeit a king of nothing.'

Everyone in the room laughed and the atmosphere lifted slightly.

'So, ladies and gentlemen, the time has come for definitive action. At first light we take Outpost Three. We'll hold it until Endellion and her party arrive later that day, then we will take the witch's head.' As Bernard spelled out the plan, there were mumblings in the room. Most, if not all, agreed. 'I'm of the belief that we *must* kill her as soon as we take her. We need to show the Azurians following her lead that we are not just a nuisance, we mean business. Also, I believe she is most dangerous, and we cannot risk her escape.'

'We can't kill her outright,' chipped in Cassandra. 'If we kill her as she is, the spell that makes her look like me will likely be broken the instant she stops breathing. Therefore, all we will have in our captivity will be a dead old crone. If we display the head of some random woman and tell them it's their queen, they're most likely to dismiss it as folly and continue the occupation.'

'I'm sorry, Prin … sorry, Bernard, I know that right now she's our greatest weapon in this war, but I'm still a little uncomfortable with the Queen of Azuria sat at our war council table,' one of the men put forth.

Cassandra nodded and stood, pushing her chair back from underneath her as she rose, gaining the attention of everyone in the room. 'I know what you all think. I know some of you consider me a spy, others among you think I *am* the witch and I've got you all under my spell. But I'll let you know this: I am hurting almost as much as any of you regarding the current states of our Kingdoms. My people have been hurt too. My family, my *direct* family, were used as pawns in this folly, some of them are *still* being used.'

'That's as maybe, Cassandra, but your kith and kin were not the ones slaughtered, made to attack each other, in your kingdom's name, were they?'

Cassandra didn't miss a beat with her response, although Bernard noticed her neck begin to shade a deep pink. 'No sir, they were not. But I hold the shame of my countrymen, the people who followed blindly a witch who twisted them around her little finger. A kingdom that has tried, and succeeded in the most part, to fulfil the genocide of another kingdom.' She paused for a moment; the man who had challenged her began to speak, but she did not allow him to interrupt her. 'Of the acts that have been perpetrated by my countrymen, I am ashamed to my bones, and I will do *everything* in my power to avenge this shame. However, I repeat, I will *not* kill my countrymen. At least not the ones who are innocent.'

'Fairly said, Cassandra, fairly said,' Bernard said, standing up, interrupting the diatribe between the two. 'Come now. We need to put our differences aside, at least for now. Cassandra has worked hard over the last year to earn the trust of me and the men of encampment two. We need to come together and work on this plan. We don't have long. Are we all agreed on this?' He offered the question to the councilman who had challenged Cassandra, and then the rest of the room.

'Agreed,' the man who had challenged her said, although Bernard thought he could see a little resentment in his eyes. *It will take time;* he thought as he watched the man fold his arms and sit back on his chair. The man looked around the room; he wasn't smiling, but his eyes told Bernard that he might come around, given time.

Shouts of agreement came from the rest of the men inside, and this filled him with hope. Maybe there *could* be a better future ahead of them.

'Agreed,' Cassandra replied when the shouts had died down. She sat and nodded towards the soldier who had challenged her. He nodded curtly in reply but kept his arms folded.

The next three hours were spent fine tuning the details of the soft approach they would be undertaking in their engagement of Outpost Three.

A plan so simple, it was brilliant.

7.

AMBRIC AND HIS Rebels were watching as a fire ripped its way through the coach house just beyond the main gate of Carnelia. The men of the watch were running around like headless chickens with buckets of water, attempting to get it under control. Up to now, their efforts had been largely fruitless. Ambric shook his head as a man, who looked vaguely familiar, threw a bottle of something onto the fire. Whatever it was caused the flames to burn higher.

Maybe he's one of ours? he thought with a chuckle.

He stayed and watched for a while with diminishing humour. He hated seeing his kingdom burn. *I suppose I should get used to it not being my kingdom anymore,* he thought, saddened. He knew it helped the morale of the men to witness these small victories, and it was good for the fight against the occupation, but ultimately, it was the slow destruction of his beloved Carnelia.

The smell from the fire wafted over their hideout. He had always enjoyed the smell of old wood burning, but not tonight. As he watched the flames grow, he could hear the men behind him rejoicing another victory. A small tear leaked from one eye and rolled down his face. He wiped it before it got lost in his beard; he didn't want to taste the salt of sorrow for what used to be his home. 'Sentimental old fool,' he scolded himself. This is what he was built for, what he had trained so hard all his life for. Not the bowing of the head or the bending of the knee stuff. For him, and his ilk, it had *always* been about death, destruction, and deception.

He turned to face his camp. His loyal men. Only half of them were soldiers. Most had been there on that day. They had watched helplessly as their sons, brothers, mothers, even grandmothers turned on each other. They watched as they were punched, kicked, bitten, or hacked to death by family, and neighbours. None of them could fathom what happened, even to this day. 'Black rain,' they would scream in the dead of night when dreams took them. 'Black rain and slow death.'

He had been too late to help. He'd only narrowly escaped the clutches of Endellion himself. When he arrived at the city, the fight—*if you could call it that*—was already over. The rains had gone, but the aftermath was there for all to see. People, good people, standing over bodies, their knuckles, mouths, eyes still dripping with Carnelian blood. He had pulled as many from the city as he could; many didn't want to leave. He created this ragtag army with the survivors.

They had quickly joined forces with Bernard's team of Ferals. Although opting to be two independent teams, their primary goals were the same. The prince had been overwhelmed to see him still alive; the last time he had seen him, Ambric had been taken by fireflies.

Even though he repeatedly told his men to stop calling him sir, he felt hypocritical every time he saw Bernard because he couldn't think of him as anything other than the Prince of Carnelia.

He rose and winced as his knees cracked into position. *Not as young as you once were, Robert,* he thought with a wry smile. 'Men,' he shouted over the muted celebration the small campfire. 'Is there any news from our friends, the Ferals?'

'Yes, Robert,' replied one of his guards. Ambric smiled as he was addressed as Robert; he liked it now. 'They say their weapon has arrived. Their plans are in place, and they're ready to strike on the crack of dawn.'

'Then let's wish them Glimm Speed.' He raised a cup that had been handed to him and gulped down the sour wine within. 'Let us also raise a toast to our friends within the walls. Tonight, was an excellent diversion to keep all eyes away from Outpost Three.'

The men cheered and drank, all of them wincing from the bitterness of the liquid.

8.

DAWN'S FIRST LIGHT broke the purple sky. The warmth of the morning, battling the dampness of the night before was causing a mist to lay low over the lands. This would be mostly burnt away by the time the sun reared its head over the mountains to cast its first full rays over the land, but for now it was a gorgeous, mysterious sight.

A caravan of weary travellers half-trotted over a hill, not ten miles from the encampment that was to be their destination. The guards on the walls watched with interest as they group reached the summit. The lookout was nervous at such a large party advancing upon the fortress, until he saw the Azurian banner flapping in the wind of the vanguard, announcing to the encampment the company approaching were friends, not foe.

The guard sent word to the Captain of the Guard, who was asleep in his chambers.

'So soon?' Captain Horatio asked. 'I knew they were in a hurry to get to Carnelia, but they must have ridden a full day and night to arrive now.'

He was up and dressed in a flash. As he arrived at the wall, he was still in the process of buttoning his jacket. 'Do we have an eye glass?' he shouted towards the men on the wall.

'Aye, sir,' came the prompt reply.

'Then use it, man. Confirm it's the queen and her guard.'

By the time Horatio had gotten to the top of the wall, he had his answer.

'Sir, I can confirm the Azurian banner, and I can confirm the identity of Queen Cassandra at the helm. I'll wager we may need to rouse the stablemen, the smithies, the cooks, and the chambermaids; they look a weary lot.'

'Thank you, sir,' Horatio replied. 'I'll attend them as you say. What estimated time of arrival do we have?'

The guard took another look through the eye glass at the group in the distance. 'At their current speed, I'd say roughly thirty minutes, sir.'

The captain barked his orders, and the men and women of service within the fortress were roused to do their duties for the incoming party.

Within the allotted time frame, everyone was present in the main courtyard, and the captain was standing before them on a small stage, erected specifically to allow him to address the crowd. He stood tall and proud, dressed in his finest uniform, as were most of the guard on active duty.

He cleared his throat, and the chatter of the crowd silenced. 'All, please note that we have incoming dignitaries. Queen Cassandra herself will be staying with us for a much-deserved rest on her long journey to the recently annexed city. I believe we have time to swap the guard of duty for her imminent arrival. Captain of the day watch, are your men ready?'

'Yes, sir, all present and correct,' came the prompt reply.

'Captain of the night watch, are you men prepared to be relieved?'

'Yes, sir, my men are ready,' came another prompt reply.

'Then you are relieved, sirs. Please attend to your duties, day watch.'

The men on the top of the wall turned and marched away in single file. They made their way down the stairs and into the main courtyard, where they met with the contingency who were about to be relieved.

A heavy BOOM, BOOM, BOOM echoed through the courtyard from the direction of the drawbridge.

'Guards, do we have identification of our party?' Captain Horatio barked his question.

There was a moment or two of complete silence. Then the shouted response came. 'Yes, sir, it is indeed our queen with her riding party, all of them verified.'

'Then lower the drawbridge and open the gates. Allow our queen the refuge of her outpost.'

'Very well, sir.' The guard on the wall shouted, as the immense metal gate began to lift. The rumble of metal grating against metal sounded like an old behemoth dying somewhere in the distance as the gate lifted from its resting place.

Once it was half-way up, the captain called his men down from the walls. It was etiquette for the full complement of the fortress to greet dignitaries on their arrival. Cassandra was sat patiently astride a white horse, which was the custom of travelling royalty of Azuria. Her entourage was filed behind her, all wearing the armour of knights of the realm. The guard at her side carried a banner.

It was the Azurian victory banner.

The queen dug her heels into the ribs of the horse she was riding, and the beast, understanding its role, took its cue and trotted into the compound. The men of her entourage followed.

As she made it into the parade ground where the guards of the fortress waited for her to address them, Captain Horatio presented himself. He was sweating and fiddling with the collar of his tunic. 'Ma'am,' he said in a self-important tone. 'It's a pleasure, and an honour, to have you here in my encampment. Your quarters have been prepared, but if I may take the liberty to ask you to be a little patient, your room is not yet fully ready. We were not expecting you for at least another twelve hours, maybe more.'

Cassandra smiled. It was filled with warmth, and the captain stopped fiddling with his collar and stood up straight. A ghost of a grin growing on his lips.

'I'm so sorry, captain. My task requires me to be in Carnelia at the earliest opportunity. We had to ride all night. It was not a fantastic prospect, what with the Rebels and the Ferals out there.'

The smile on Horatio's face blossomed, and all evidence of his nervousness left him. 'I assure you, ma'am, we have had no issue with that band of scum here. These walls are fortified. Now, if there is anything I can do to make your rest here more pleasurable, please say the word and it shall be done.'

Queen Cassandra smiled again. There was a playful glint in her eye, one that was even a little flirty. 'Oh yes, captain, there's one small thing you can do for me ...'

His cheeks bloomed a light pink, and he toyed with the neck of his tunic again. 'Please, Your Highness, just name it.'

A shout arose from the guardsmen who had followed the queen into the fortress. It was loud and unexpected, taking Captain Horatio by surprise. He snapped from his small, romantic daydream regarding him and Queen Cassandra, and physically jumped. As he did, a man stepped out from behind the queen and grabbed him by the arm. The grip was tight.

'What's the meaning of this? Unhand me at once,' he snapped. 'I'll have your warrant for this insubordination.'

As the shouts from around the fortress continued, many faces appeared over the top of the walls. Horatio looked up, not completely understanding what was happening. As the faces on the walls became bodies, he saw they were carrying their own banners.

The banners of The Ferals.

'Well, Captain,' Cassandra continued. 'I'd like you to explain to me how safe your walls are one more time. Oh, and I would also like you to surrender this encampment to us.' She gestured towards the men on the top of the walls, surrounding the guard within the courtyard. She continued her gesture towards the men who had followed her inside the fortress. 'It would seem the Feral scum have completely outsmarted you, Captain. Now, my question to you is, do you yield?'

Horatio's wide eyes left the smiling blue ones of Cassandra and looked around his courtyard. His mouth hung wide as his gaze took in everything happening around him. The Ferals on the wall drew their weapons; broadswords, spears, bows and arrows were produced and directed at his men. Finally, his gaze fell back upon Cassandra. 'Why, my queen?' he stuttered.

'Because, at this moment in time, I am not the queen you think I am. You're following the lead of a witch who killed your real queen, my mother.' Cassandra bowed her head but continued to speak. 'Now, I have no appetite to kill my own countrymen, Captain, but I will if you do not yield. So, I ask you once again. Do you yield?'

Captain Horatio took a deep breath and visibly wobbled. 'We yield,' he replied in hushed tones. As the words fell from his mouth, Cassandra raised her hand and all the Ferals in the courtyard, and on the walls, cheered. The Azurian guard laid down their weapons, and interlaced their fingers at the back of their heads, assuming the surrender position.

D E McCluskey

9.

THE NIGHT BEFORE Cassandra and The Ferals took Outpost Three, Endellion and her party rode into Outpost Two to rest prior to their penultimate ride towards Carnelia. The moment the gate was up and they were safely within the grounds, she dismounted her white horse. The Captain of the Guard had greeted her, with all his men in attendance.

'Ma'am, it is an honour to have you under our—'

He never got to finish his welcome as she raised a hand, dismissing him. He stopped talking instantly and watched as she walked off in the direction of the bunting that had been raised to welcome her.

I must confront the Glimm, she thought as she struggled with the latch of her cloak. *There's something tasking me about the purple ...*

She ran through the doors and up the stairs, following the gay decor and the flowers that had been laid out for her. She came to a large door that was guarded by two men dressed in battle uniform. Neither flinched as she stormed up the corridor towards them. 'Are these my chambers?' she snapped.

One of them looked at her; his face devoid of emotion. 'It is, ma'am,' he grumbled in a voice that sounded like thunder rumbling in a summer sky.

'Well, let me in and make yourselves scarce. I need privacy for the next hour.'

'Yes, ma'am,' the guard grumbled again.

Endellion watched as they walked off slowly down the corridor towards the stairs she had just ascended. When she was satisfied they were gone, she let herself into the chambers, locking the door behind her.

~~~~

Alexander was running up the stairs to find her when he bumped into the two guards. 'Where are you going, prince?' the gravelly voiced guard asked.

'I need to see my sister. Did she pass you?'

'Yes, she did, but she gave us strict orders that no one should pass into the chambers for one hour.'

'I'm her brother, her prince. I must see her,' he demanded, looking up at the two men towering over him.

'Not now, Prince Alexander, she is resting.'

Alexander tried his best to hustle past them, but they were too large for him to even get a sight of his sister's door. The two men looked at each other before picking the protesting prince up by his armpits. They then proceeded to march him down the steps, back into the courtyard.

'I'll have your heads for this,' he screamed. 'This is treason, I tell you. Treason.' Tears were growing fat in his eyes, but still the guards barred his access. He looked towards the window of the room in which he knew his sister, his queen, was currently residing. A faint red glow emanated from behind the curtains. He was frustrated and angry that he couldn't be there for her.

~~~~~

Inside the chambers, Endellion had reverted to her true form. She had stretched, and rolled her neck, relishing the relief of her bones cracking back into place. The glowing Glimmer was nestling safely in her hands as she sat cross legged in the centre of the room. Her eyes were closed, but her mouth was forming words.

'Tell me, old man, tell me of the purple,' she demanded. 'Has it anything to do with the second Glimmer?'

In the ruins of the old temple, one of the three men with the beards was smiling as he spoke. 'Of the Glimmers, there are two, search your heart, you know it's true; trust your feeling, use your head, one is blue, the other red.'

Endellion's rage came forth unexpectedly, even to her. 'Why are you talking to me in childish rhymes?' she screamed. 'Why will you not give me an answer?'

'I just did,' the old man replied without a flinch at her anger.

She rushed at him, screaming, her fingers clawed, her long, cracked fingernails lethal weapons. The old man didn't move; he merely watched as she yelled and clawed at him. Every time her hands swung, they swooped through him as if he was a dream, which, of course, he was. Realising her attack was futile, she turned her attentions to the two skeletons on the altar. She tried to grab one of them, wanting to drag it from its resting place, wanting to throw it, to smash it, to shred its millennia-aged bones to the four corners of the chamber; but once again, her hands passed through them.

She opened her eyes into the real world. Her anger and rage were still very much within her, but her body showed no signs of it. Slowly, she looked at the red ball glowing in her hands. Her breathing sped up, and her heart began pacing—it felt like it was bouncing like a child's ball against her ribs. She opened her mouth and roared. It was a deep, primal sound that carried like it came from somewhere deeper than her stomach, maybe from her soul. She gripped the glowing ball in her hands and threw it.

It hit the wall with a dull, anti-climactic thud.

The red glow instantly dimmed, and the orb became nothing but a small grey ball.

Her eyes widened when she realised what she had done. With a gasp, she scrambled to her feet, using the post of the bed as a crutch, and flung herself towards the wall where the Glimmer rested. Cradling the orb, she ran her fingers over its surface, working them into a frenzy, searching for any cracks or dents. When none were found, she realised she had been holding her breath the whole time and released it slowly. Relieved, but still furious with the Glimm, she sat back onto the floor and closed her eyes. She rubbed her fingers over the ball and whispered, 'Fireflies, to me.'

A low vibration filled the room, and a light *tap, tap, tap* from the window caught caused her to smile. She stood, more composed now pulled back the curtain. Her eyes fell upon one of the most beautiful sights she had seen in a long time. A single mutated firefly was hovering at her window. Its thorax aglow with a sickly-sweet golden light. The large, deadly sting at the bottom of its bloated abdomen was glistening.

'Ah, my pretty thing,' she purred, opening the window allowing the beast inside. 'What have you to report of my path towards Carnelia?'

~~~~

From the now deserted courtyard, Alexander could hear the familiar buzz of the fireflies. He watched from his hidden location opposite his sister's dwelling as the red glow was replaced with a golden one. His shoulders fell as his body relaxed. He knew she was safe now, in the company of her fireflies. A smile spread on his lips as he got up and made his way inside to stand guard outside his sister's chambers.

10.

ROBERT AMBRIC WAS reading the note of parchment that had arrived on the leg of a dark raven. He hated the arrival of these birds as they very rarely brought good news. It was usually the death of a family member or an attack somewhere in the wild woods that he would need to clean up. But not this time. This time the bird did bring good news. Well, good news to him and his Rebels. It was regarding Outpost Three. He smiled as he read the words, marvelling at how fast Bernard and his Ferals had taken the encampment.

Still holding the parchment, he marched into camp. The men were busy taking down tents, washing pots, and covering up the fire. Most of them noticed his urgency as he stormed into the centre. 'Men,' he shouted, getting the attention of the others who were not looking his way. 'Today we march to Outpost Three. There seems to be, maybe three-hundred prisoners there who need to be taken care of.' It took a few moments for this information to sink in, but when it did, a cheer ripped through the gathering. 'By the dawn of tomorrow, the witch Endellion, the sacker of Carnelia, will be in our hands.' Another cheer tore through the camp. He smiled as he surveyed his men. 'Carnelia will be free once again!'

It felt strange to smile.

Good, but still strange.

11.

ENDELLION AWOKE ALONE in her chambers. She had fallen asleep in the centre of the room, her Glimmer on the floor next to her. She picked it up in haste and examined it, remembering what she had done in her fury last night. Even though she knew it still worked—she had communicated with a firefly, and it was still in her thrall—she was desperate to give it a second inspection. *I must control my temper*, she thought.

As she went to open her chamber door, she caught a glimpse of herself in the full-length mirror over the other side of the room. She was surprised, and aghast, to find herself in her original guise. As she considered the mirror, the aged and greying Endellion stared back at her. The vision almost caused her to yell, as she was expecting to see the youthful Cassandra. *Where is my head at?* she questioned herself. *I almost walked out of the queen's chamber as a stranger.*

She wrapped her fingers around the glimmer again and closed her eyes. A wind whipped her and her hair began to shine as the features of her face morphed into someone else, someone younger. Eventually, she opened her eyes, and the beauty of Cassandra smiled at her from the mirror. She nodded and continued to the door.

As she opened it, Alexander fell inside with a grunt. He'd been asleep, leaning on the wood for support. With a tut, and a roll of her eyes, she prodded him with her foot.

'My prince,' she whispered. 'Come inside my chambers and continue your slumber in comfort.' She feigned a small giggle, as if the presence of him had amused her, when in reality it had done the opposite.

A startled Alexander rubbed his eyes and looked at her. 'Cass,' he grunted, still half asleep. 'I … I stood watch as you consulted your fireflies. I didn't want anyone else guarding you. But I'm sorry, I must have fallen asleep.'

Endellion mustered her inner actress and smiled a fake Cassandra smile at the interfering little brat at her feet. 'That's OK, brother,' she replied, hoping the contempt she felt couldn't be heard. 'You go continue your sleep. I have much to do.'

'I thought we were in a hurry to get to Carnelia?' Alexander asked, as he made his way, stumbling as if drunk, into the chambers and towards the comfortable looking bed.

'Things have changed. There's not so much urgency now. We'll take our leave at leisure,' she replied. 'I'll return within a few hours. You sleep now, I'm going to need you at full strength today.'

76

She left the boy fighting with the blankets on her unruffled bed. She had unfinished business to conduct concerning her personal quest for the Throne of Glimm. As she left the room, the two guards stationed outside the door snapped to attention. She started to walk off down the corridor, but they followed her. She stopped and turned to look at the soldiers, who had stopped behind her. She rolled her eyes and continued; the soldiers continued walking too. 'You two, you don't have to follow me.'

Neither soldier spoke, they just stood, staring ahead down the corridor where she was heading.

Endellion stared at them. 'You're dismissed,' she snapped.

The men ignored her, continuing to stare ahead of her. She huffed and walked off again. The soldiers followed. She needed to consult the Glimm, and to do this, she needed privacy.

An idea popped into her head.

She took the stairs into the courtyard, closely followed by the two soldiers, and made her way towards the officers' mess. As she stormed inside, all the soldiers stopped what they were doing and stood.

'Which of you is the captain of the guards?' she ordered.

A large man with a thick brown beard stood up. He straightened his tunic and wiped food from his mouth. 'My queen, I'm the Captain of the Guards. Captain Varthos, at your service,' he offered, slightly out of breath.

'Captain, are your personal chambers secure?'

The large man's eyes regarded her; they were the eyes of a man who didn't know what to do, or what to say. 'Erm, yes, my lady,' he stuttered.

She smiled at him. 'Good, then I'm commandeering them for a short while. I am *not* to be interrupted, not for anything, do you understand?'

'Yes, of course. I'll accompany you to them now.'

'Thank you, captain.'

The big man looked around the room as if he was looking for someone to tell him how he should react to this situation. Once he realised he was on his own, he wiped his mouth again and stepped away from the table. 'Erm, well, this way, Your Majesty.'

'Captain Varthos, are you in charge of my royal guard?'

'I am.'

'Please tell them to stand down. I can't be having them following me everywhere I go.'

'They are there for your own protection, Your Majesty,' he replied.

'Sir, I am inside a fortress. I came accompanied by one hundred and fifty of my very own men; you have a further three hundred stationed within this compound. What could possibly happen to me here?'

Varthos raised his finger, ready to answer her query before he realised she wasn't looking for an answer. Instead, he pointed towards the two guards and signalled for them to move away, which they dully did.

'Thank you,' she smiled. 'Now, if you would lead the way.'

They walked from the officer's mess and along a winding corridor. Eventually, Varthos stopped outside of large, lavish door.

'These are my quarters. I'm sure you'll find them to your satisfaction,' he said, opening the door, allowing her inside.

'I'm sure I will,' she replied. 'You may leave me now. I need total and utter solitude. No one is to interrupt me. Do you understand?' she asked.

He nodded as Endellion, in Cassandra's disguise, entered the room.

The chambers were large but sparsely decorated. *These will do perfectly,* she thought.

Once the captain left and she had locked the door behind her, she reverted to her natural form. Removing the Glimmer from her pocket, she sat cross legged in the centre of the room. As her eyes closed, the Glimmer began to glow its dark red as she was transported back into the altar room.

~~~~

It didn't matter how ghastly she was to the men of the Glimm, if she held the Glimmer, they were honour bound to help her in any way they could.

'My lady, how may we be of help today?' one of the three bearded men before her asked.

'I need to find the Throne of Glimm,' she stated. 'And I require your help in this quest.'

'You already know where it is … my lady,' another said, a hint of a smug smile on his face

'I do?' Endellion asked. Her eyes narrowed as she scrutinised the man who had spoken. She had never known these men to have a sense of humour before. Her brow ruffled as she leaned towards them. 'Is this another of your cryptic answers?'

'No, my lady. A long time ago, you were in considerable trouble. The Glimmer that you hold in your hand was attracted to your purple. It helped you, you just didn't know it.'

Endellion shook her head. 'When was this? When did I get help from the Throne of Glimm?' she demanded, her voice dripping with anger.

'It was a long time ago.'

Endellion hissed and shooed away the very idea of what the Glimm had uttered. 'You talk rubbish, man.'

'He is correct,' the man on the left spoke…

PART 3

1.

KING LEOPOLD AND Queen Rabia were sat at the hearth in their living chambers. The fire in the pit was roaring, casting its orange glow around the darkened room, creating strange dancing shadows on the walls that were entertaining. The smell of the maple bark burning was sweet, and the occasional pop of a knot in the wood added to the relaxed, cosy atmosphere in the room.

The heavy snows had come, and the Kingdom of Carnelia had been laid siege beneath a blanket of pretty whiteness. The children, of course, loved it, thrilling in the delights of snowball fights and sledging down the steep hills outside the walls. However, the farmers and the old folk detested it. It brought ruined crops and fields, it brought floods, but most of all, it brought death.

Prince Thaddius and Lady Endellion were playing together on a shaggy mat made from the hide of a large bear that King Leopold professed he had trapped and killed. The truth of the matter was it was one of his men, Bob Ambric, who had trapped it. All Leopold had done was deliver the final blow to the defenceless animal.

The children, not long turned six-years-old, were enjoying the warmth of the fire.

The queen was sat in her reading chair, a book open on her lap. But she was not reading, there was more entertainment in watching the children play. 'Just look at them, Leo. Playing nicely together. They really could be brother and sister.' A small wistful smile broke on her lips, and her gaze seemed to float off into the ether.

'Well, as long as you remember they're not, then there'll be no problems,' Leopold replied grumpily from his seat, where he was busy eating a large sandwich off a small plate. 'And don't be getting any romantic ideas about marriage between them either. You have to remember that she is *lowborn*, and as a lowborn woman, she is not eligible to marry into royalty.'

'I know all of that. Why do you feel the need to bring it up each time I mention them having fun together?'

The king looked at the children giggling and rolling on the rug. His mouth grimaced, and he looked like one who had taken a long drink of warm, sour milk. 'I'm sorry, Rabia.' He shook his head. 'I just cannot take to the child.' *Every time I look at her, she reminds me of what I did*, he added to himself. His mind conjured the image of Camarilla's lifeless face, with her pale skin and blue lips, her lifeless eyes looking up at him, through him, accusing him.

He shuddered at the thought.

As he did, Endellion stopped her game and looked up at him.

Her dark eyes stared intently for a long moment, too long for Leopold's liking. She held this stare without blinking or smiling.

The king's face turned from revulsion to fear.

His physical features stayed the same, but his eyes widened, and he felt the hairs on the back of his neck begin to prickle as a terrifying thought passed through his mind. *Can she read my thoughts?* He put his sandwich down on the table next to him and sat back in the chair, not taking his eyes off the strange girl.

Then her face softened. She flashed him a sweet smile and resumed her game.

Rabia, unaware of Leopold's scare, stood from her chair and bent over the children. 'What are you playing there, my lovelies?' she asked kindly.

'We're playing battles, Mother,' Thaddius replied with the cute, high-pitched tone that she loved so much.

'Battles, eh? Who's winning?'

'I'm blue and Thaddius is red,' Endellion replied, her voice just as cute as the prince's. 'And over here, we have the purples. They're the ones who don't want to fight. The lady told me the purple ones are the strongest.'

Queen Rabia cocked her head to the side and narrowed her eyes. 'What lady, dear?' she asked.

'Oh, just the one in my dreams,' the child answered, already looking bored with the conversation and returning to her game. Then, almost as if she'd forgotten an important detail, she looked back at Rabia. Her eyes were wide and innocent, and there was the merest hint of a smile on her face. 'She has purple skin, you know.'

'Purple skin? Come now, Endellion, you know there are no such people who have purple skin. That's some imagination you have,' Rabia laughed.

'My mother did. The purple lady told me.'

The queen recoiled as if she had been slapped in the face. There had been no talk of Camarilla for years, and she'd almost forgotten about her strange hospital friend.

On hearing the talk regarding the little girl's mother, King Leopold had had enough. He put his sandwich down on the plate again and stood up. The queen already knew he was serious, as Leopold never disturbed his eating for anything. He crossed to where the children were playing and stood over them, his arms behind his back.

'Come now, children,' he said assertively, instantly getting the attention of the two friends. 'It's well past your bedtimes. You both have schooling in the morning, and I don't want you to be tired, there's a lot to learn. You can wash up and then it's off to your individual chambers.'

Both children groaned their displeasure at this news but knew any resistance would be futile. Once the king had made up his mind, that was that.

He rang a small bell that was beside the fire, and a servant girl entered the room. 'Please, Molly,' the king addressed the newcomer. 'Take these two scallywags off to bed. Make sure they wash first; they've been playing in front of that fire for hours.'

The young girl nodded, curtsied, and ushered the children out of the room.

Once they were alone, Rabia turned towards her husband and scowled. 'Leopold, don't you think that that was a trifle mean?'

The king shuddered. It was small on the outside, but it shook him to the bone on the inside.

He scowled at his wife. 'No, not at all, woman. It's dark, cold, and late. They must be up early tomorrow, there is a long day of schooling ahead of them, they could do with an early night. Besides, all that talk of purple skinned ladies in dreams, I ask you …' He sat back down on his chair, eyeing the remains of his sandwich. He considered picking it back up and finishing it, but his appetite had dwindled. He pushed the plate away from him and sat back in his chair. His mind already elsewhere.

The queen watched the quandary regarding the sandwich with a mixture of humour and alarm. Leopold never left half a sandwich uneaten. She reopened her book but kept an eye on her troubled husband.

~~~~

Later that night, when everyone was in bed, Leopold was tossing and turning. His brain refusing to switch off. When he did manage to catch a snippet of sleep, strange dreams troubled him.

He was in the hospital. The stink of disinfectant and death hung heavily in the air of the darkened room. He could taste it on the back of his throat. The heat and closeness of the room caused pressure within his head, and it throbbed in tandem with the beating of his heart. He rubbed his eyes, attempting to relieve some of that pressure, but it was to no avail. When he opened them again, he was surprised to see two beds before him. One contained his beloved wife, the other a wretch of a woman. He knew it was Camarilla, but it didn't look like her. There was a purple hue to her skin. He didn't know if this was due to her loss of blood or something else entirely.

He watched as thick, dark liquid transferred from the wretch into his wife via a tube. The way it crawled through the vessel into Rabia's arm sickened him. There was something about it, something otherworldly that he detested. His mouth narrowed to a thin white line as the liquid continued to seep.

The last of the blood drained from the purple woman into his wife. He marvelled as he watched Rabia's skin change from a dull, lifeless white to a healthy, warm pink. A voice from somewhere around him spoke; it was deep and resonant.

'The transfusion is complete. You may remove the needle,' it boomed.

He watched, detached, as his own hands gripped the needle, yanking it from the purple woman's arm. As he did, her hand grabbed him. It made him jump. The grip was solid, and he could feel her strong, icy fingers tighten around his wrist. With wide eyes, he looked down at the lifeless body on the bed. Her eyes flickered open, and a wicked smile spread across her face.

'You'll do well to look after her, Leopold. Or she will be the undoing of your nation. Fear The Great Lord Glimm,' she said. Her voice was a whisper, but it sounded like there were several people speaking, all at the same time.

The cacophony petrified Leopold, and he pulled away from the horrific creature on the bed. Her eyes narrowed. He could feel his bladder weakening as her dead, purple lips grinned, splitting the skin, and exposing sharp, yellow teeth. Then, she closed her eyes and fell back into death's embrace.

Leopold bolted upright in his bed. His frantic eyes searched the darkened room. It took more than a few moments to realise he was no longer in the hospital, that he was safe in the sanctuary of his chambers. His heart pounded in his throat, and the cooling damp of his sweat was seeping into the pillow behind him.

'It was only a dream,' he whispered, smiling and shaking his head. He turned his pillow over from the wet side to the dry. As he fluffed it, a strange sensation pained his forearm. He clenched and unclenched his fist, stretching the tendons. Looking down in the gloom of the darkened room, he thought he could see four long, dark bruises forming.

The bruises looked like fingers.

~~~~

That morning, the royal family was up early and eating breakfast together. It had become a tradition, more for the queen's sake than the king's, for Endellion to be invited to their table for meals. Thaddius was always pleased she was there.

The king had awoken in a foul mood and had grumbled and grunted his way through the whole meal. His eyes darker, more brooding than usual, and Rabia could see bags beneath them.

'What ails you this morning, my love?' she asked. 'It seemed you were having the most awful dreams last night. You tossed and turned, shouting out indecipherable screams.'

'I'm fine, my wife. I have a few things on my mind is all. Now, pray, if you would leave me in peace with my thoughts, all will be well.'

The queen smiled and patted his hand. 'Very well, my dear,' she said, getting up and placing her napkin on the table before her. She turned her attentions on the children, who were whispering and giggling.

They were playing a game that involved shaking their fists three times and producing an item; the item would either be paper, scissors, or a rock; the winner would be decided on whose item could destroy the other. As they started a new game, they began to giggle loudly, as children do. Leopold was resting his elbow on the table, with his forehead buried in the palm of his hand. He took in a deep breath and glared at the rowdy children.

'You two,' he roared. 'I'll not ask again for you both to be quiet while I eat. I do not want to hear another peep out of either of you. Do you understand me?'

The children jumped at the severity of the yell and fell silent in an instant. Their faces looked at the king with wide eyes, wide mouths, and flailing nostrils. Endellion's eyes were filling with tears as she held her small fist towards the prince; she had been intent on producing the rock within the game.

Rabia had also been taken by surprise by the ferocity of his rant. 'Leopold,' she scolded. 'There's no reason to raise your voice to the children in that way. They are only playing.'

As Rabia defended them, Endellion dropped her fist, inadvertently hitting the bowl of oats place before her. The bowl flipped into the air, the oats and the milk spilling and splashing everywhere, including over the king.

The warmed cereal burned him as it landed.

'WHAT IS THIS OUTRAGE?' he screamed, slamming his own fists on the table, making the rest of the dishes dance. As he jumped from his chair, the oats and hot milk dripping from his beard, he reached for the terrified young girl, grabbing her by her arm. He noticed with some clarity through his rage that he grabbed the child in the same place he had been grabbed by her mother in his dream the previous night.

D E McCluskey

Endellion began to scream in fear of the angry adult looming over her. This, in turn, caused Thaddius to cry. Leopold's fury doubled as he saw his son's tears, and he raised his hand. He paused for a moment, as if questioning what he was about to do, but it was only a moment. He brought his hand down hard across Endellion's face. The force of the slap knocked her to the ground. He had done this with more strength than he meant to. His breath was coming hard and fast, and thick white spittle had formed in the corners of his lips. He then turned to his son.

'Thaddius,' he demanded. The boy turned towards him, his face ashen and his eyes wide. 'You are *not* to play with this … this … lowborn daughter of a whore again. Do you hear me? DO YOU HEAR ME, BOY?'

Thick tears were flowing down Thaddius's cheeks as he nodded his understanding. Overcompensating in case he would be next for the beating.

'Now, all of you be gone and leave me in peace,' he bellowed as he wiped the cooling oats from his face and tunic.

Horrified by what had just happened, Rabia turned from glaring at her husband and looked towards the children. She caught sight of Endellion as she ran off, out of the dining room and into the corridor. Rabia tutted and shook her head at a defiant Leopold, before giving chase.

The six-year-old was fast, too fast for her to catch as she exited the dining room. She was gone. Rabia followed along the corridor, calling her name.

~~~~

Endellion watched Rabia pass from a small hiding space beneath a long sideboard adorning one of the walls, halfway down the corridor. The girl's hand was held to her stinging face, as if to stifle the sobs spilling from her. Her face stung where the king had struck her, and her arm throbbed from where he had grabbed her. She didn't want the queen to hear her hiding there, as she would probably want to hit her too.

She wanted to stay hidden forever.

After a short while, the fear and anxiety began to drain from her, leaving her body tired, and she fell into a doze.

She assumed it had been a doze, as the purple skinned woman was there again. She looked familiar, almost as if she were looking into a mirror, a mirror that could see into the future. The main difference between her and the purple skinned woman was that she thought the woman looked sad. *I suppose I look sad now too,* she thought.

With a melancholic smile, the purple woman beckoned Endellion to follow her. She felt she had no choice in the matter and did as she was bid. As she climbed out of her hiding place, she expected her arms and legs to scream in protest, complaining about how long that they had been cooped up in such a small place; but they didn't. She rose from underneath the unit, and the purple woman held her hand out towards her.

Endellion knew her. She knew there she had a special bond with her, even though she had never seen her outside of her dreams. With a warm but confusing smile, the woman led her down a corridor she had never seen before. It was dark and dusty, and even though the little girl knew this to be a dream, she could smell must and dampness in the air. It was the smell of age and neglect.

Endellion was scared. She had never been to such an old and decrepit part of the castle before. She closed her eyes as she passed through a spider's web decorating the passage from ceiling to the floor. *They must be huge spiders to create such webs,* she thought. The purple woman passed through them, leaving them undisturbed.

She turned and beckoned Endellion to follow her.

The small girl swallowed. The sweat in the palms of her hands was cold in the dank air, but she felt she had no other choice but to follow this … *ghost?* through the uninviting corridor.

The woman stopped roughly halfway down. As she turned and regarded Endellion, the sad smile was back on her lips. She pointed to the floor, and a flood of purple light began to ebb from her body. It filled the corridor with a magical light that encompassed Endellion and everything else in its glow.

The girl's eyes didn't want to leave the vision of the woman, but reluctantly, she tore them from their fixation and looked towards the location to which the lady was pointing. In the glow, Endellion could make out a slight depression in the floor. Her heart was racing, pounding with the promise of adventure, equalled with the greatest fear she had ever felt in her life.

She wished Thaddius had been here to enjoy this with her, but most of all, she wished him here just for the company.

Not entirely sure if it was the right thing to do, she went to the indentation and, using her fingertips, pulled at the old, musty carpet. It was ugly to her touch, almost as if it was damp with rot. The stink was almost physical. It reminded her of the boys who worked with the horses when her and Thaddius went riding. Biting her lip, she dug her fingernails deeper into the old carpet and pulled. The tiles moved ever so slightly. With a look over her shoulder to see if there was anyone other than the purple woman watching, she continued her work, satisfied they were alone.

It took a small while for her to shift the carpet. Her hands and knees were filthy from the work. Wiping the sheen of sweat from her forehead left a swathe of dirt across her face as the last piece of carpet finally gave way. The cause of the indentation in the floor was revealed. It was a trap door.

She looked at the silent, glowing woman as if seeking permission to open it.

With a sad smile, the woman gave it, nodding her head towards the youth. Endellion wiped the filth and sweat covering her hands before grasping the rusted metal ring, acting as the handle, and pulled with all her might.

It was heavy, but it finally began to give. It wasn't long before the door was open enough for her to slide her fingers beneath and pull it the rest of the way. Eventually, the trapdoor opened, revealing a hole as black as she imagined death itself to be.

The purple skinned woman floated towards it, lighting the darkness inside with her strange luminescence. She indicated for Endellion to follow her down into the darkness.

She didn't want to.

She was scared of the spiders and the rats and any other monstrosities that might lurk in a castle's dungeon, one that didn't look like it had been accessed in hundreds of years.

However, her guide was insistent.

Endellion thought disobeying a ghost was not a good idea, no matter how odd or scary the request was. With this in mind, she reluctantly entered the abyss before her.

The steps led down to a tunnel. The ghost continued along it, beckoning her to follow. She did so, wanting to either close her eyes or to wake up from this strange dream in the safety of her chambers, ready for another day of playing with her best friend in the world.

Neither of those things happened.

The further along the tunnel she looked, she noticed the walls changing from cut stone and concrete to rock, then eventually to earth and clay. The light from the glowing woman before her informed her they were travelling downwards.

After what seemed like a long and arduous journey, the tunnel ended abruptly, flowing into a huge chamber. It was darker in here than it had been in the tunnel, even when the purple woman floated in with her radiance. Her light couldn't penetrate deep into the oppressive void.

Eventually, her eyes adjusted to the new darkness and shadows began to form around her. From what she could see, it looked like a different version of the Great Hall, but one that was much older.

With a wave of her hand, the woman illuminated a throne, of sorts, and several small but long benches that formed a crude circle. As her glowing guide floated along the walls, she revealed drawings and carvings within the stone and clay. They depicted old men in gowns and long beards. In some of the drawings, the men were holding something in their hands, something small and round. The imagery indicated the orb was glowing. It looked like the things contained power, a power that the men holding them revered. The other men in the drawings, the ones who looked like savages, were shying away from them as if scared.

The purple skinned woman smiled in a familiar way that made Endellion feel more reassured than she thought she should. For some reason, she trusted this woman, almost as if she were family.

The thought of family made Endellion feel sad.

How the king had shouted and how the queen had run after her, made her realise, even at such a young age, that she did not belong where she lived. She felt the king barely even tolerated her.

The glowing woman's face changed when she saw sadness creeping into Endellion's face, and she attempted to reach out, to touch her, but something off to the side, where Endellion couldn't see, stopped her. The woman nodded and retracted her hand. Instead, she pointed towards the throne in the centre of the room.

Endellion followed the gesture and went and sat on the large seat. She liked the way it felt beneath her as she wriggled to get comfortable on the odd structure. An unexpected rush of power surged through her.

As she sat, the drawings of the men with the beards became illuminated from an unknown, and unseen, source. The purple woman was floating next to her, so she knew it couldn't have been from her.

The drawings began to make sense.

She could see they were arranged in a pattern depicting a story. Endellion had always loved picture books, especially ones that told true stories, and she recognised the configuration straight away.

They depicted a visit by a single man, a man with long white hair and robes. Studying them further, she was thrilled to notice that it looked like the man had visited the very place where she was sitting now, this very room. He had met with the king, or at least the leader of this place, and offered him a gift.

The carvings clearly depicted the old man handing over a small glowing ball. In the next picture, the king was accepting the gift, and the people around had fallen to their knees. The next one showed the bearded man standing with his arms raised and everyone looking to him in awe.

He then left.

Saddened at the end of the story, Endellion noticed there were other, smaller drawings on the walls.

It looked as if the old man had been followed.

A kind of map had been drawn, depicting what looked to her as a long journey ending somewhere within a huge castle, with a great altar. There, the man met with someone who was drawn with the same likeness as him. The two men embraced before promptly killing each other on an altar.

Suddenly, she didn't like sitting on this throne anymore. She jumped up and raced past the purple skinned woman and back up the tunnel.

Once back in the castle, she closed the hatch and ran to her bedchambers. There, she jumped on her bed, covered her head with her blankets, and promptly fell asleep.

~~~~

When she awoke, a few hours later, late for school and knowing she would be in even more trouble than she was already, her head was still reeling from the odd dream.

As she made her way into the bathroom to get ready for whatever punishment was coming her way, she looked at herself in the mirror.

She was surprised to find herself covered in dirt and cobwebs.

2.

BACK ON THE floor in the captain's quarters in Carnelian Outpost Two, Endellion opened her eyes. Her face, her original face, looked alive as her smile came to fruition. 'I knew it …' she whispered aloud. 'I knew there was a reason I needed to return to Carnelia.'

Tucking the Glimmer back into the folds of her dress, she got up from the floor, exited the room, and ran through the fortress, towards her own chambers. She needed to rouse Alexander.

'Alex! Brother, I need you to wake up? We have to leave right now,' she gasped, struggling to catch her breath.

The boy rubbed his eyes as he stirred awake. He looked at the strange woman who had roused him from his sleep and was leaning over him, shaking him. Once his sleep addled brain caught up with him, his face changed, and his eyes narrowed at the stranger.

'Who are you?' he shouted, jumping up off the bed. 'What are you doing in the queen's chambers?' He dashed for his long sword, which was resting on the chair on the other side of the room, next to his clothes.

Endellion cursed. *How could I have forgotten to change back into Cassandra's form? I'm getting clumsy,* she thought. Her eyes scanned the room as she wracked her brain for an excuse. 'Pardon me, sire,' she stuttered, putting on a high-pitched voice, 'but her Highness, Queen Cassandra, sent me to rouse you from your sleep. She ordered me inform you that your party will be leaving promptly. She wants you to ready the riding party for a full night's ride. She wants to reach Carnelia's annex, post haste.' She added a curtsey at the last minute and dropped her gaze.

Alexander was halfway across the room when he stopped to look at her. He looked to be more embarrassed that he was in his underwear in front of a stranger than he was angry at her intrusion. 'Where is my sister now?' he demanded, picking up his trousers.

'She commandeered the captain's quarters, my Lord. She's there now, finishing her work and getting herself ready for the ride. That's why she sent me to you.'

'Very well,' the boy replied, slipping his legs into the trousers quicker than he intended to do. He knocked his sword from the chair where it was resting and jerked forward, attempting to stop it from hitting the floor. He looked up at the stranger, his face flushed and red. 'I'll bathe and then inform the riding party to mount for imminent departure. Thank you, my lady.'

'You're welcome, young sire,' she said, bowing before him. 'Is there anything else?'

'No.' He dismissed her with a wave of his hand. 'Go back to your duties,' he snapped, turning towards the bathroom.

~~~~~

As he heard the door close behind him, he was struck with a feeling that he had met that woman before. He narrowed his eyes, trying to think what it was about her that was so familiar. He shook his head and continued into the bathroom to draw himself a bath.

As he lay in the warm water, a single thought troubled him. *Why did she call me brother when she was trying to wake me?*

3.

OUTPOST THREE WAS buzzing with Ferals, all of them wearing the uniforms of the captured Azurian Guards, busy putting their trap together for the arrival tonight of Endellion and her guards. The prisoners, all of them wearing civilian clothing, were lined up in the courtyard. They were awaiting Robert Ambric's arrival and their subsequent removal from the fortress.

Cassandra and Bernard were alone in a meeting room, on the opposite ends of a long wooden table. They were deep in discussion, addressing the issue of what they should do with Endellion when she arrived.

'I'm thinking the men have a point. She should be killed immediately. Who knows what else she's capable of if left unchecked?' Bernard argued this point with his head in his hands.

'I understand what you're saying, but do we bring ourselves down to her level if we murder her in cold blood?' Cassandra replied. 'Shouldn't we give her a chance to explain herself first?'

'It's hardly cold blood, is it? She's out there killing, and sacking, in the name of Azuria. She's using your face and your banner. If she can impersonate you so well that even your own brother cannot tell you apart, then who knows what else she can do with her dark magic.'

Cassandra shook her head. She was attempting to weigh up the pros and cons of both sides of this argument. 'OK.' The word finally broke the silence in the room. 'I see your point regarding what she can do, but what are we going to do regarding her riders? They're loyal men of Azuria acting on what they believe is the best interests of their kingdom.'

'Once we have her in custody, we will prove to them they've been duped by a witch. Once we remove her head and she reverts to her natural form, we'll display it for the riders to see. To see who, or what, they have been following for the last year.'

'I won't have my countrymen killed for no reason. But, if they're still resistant after we've proved them otherwise, and if they become violent, then, and only then, do we consider the alternative. Agreed?' Cassandra asked, bowing her head low.

Bernard's face was a dichotomy of emotions. He was trying his best to look sympathetic to her cause, but he knew, and he thought she did too, it would be an up-hill battle convincing his men not to kill the Azurian riders after what they had witnessed and the stories of atrocities within Carnelia after the sacking.

He lowered his head and shook it. 'Agreed,' he conceded.

'OK then,' Cassandra said, standing up from the table. 'Let us prepare for the end of this stinking occupation.'

Bernard smiled at the uplift in her voice.

'The men are dressing in the uniform of Azuria from the captured men,' Bernard explained. 'You need to know that every man who is a Feral will have a small red line painted down the left-hand side of their armour. Should it come to it, it should be enough to differentiate between them. Although, we *are* hoping that battle will not commence,' Bernard warned.

'Let's pray to the Glimm that it doesn't,' she said with a smile. She walked around the table, towards where he was sitting. She wrapped her arms around his neck, leaned in, and gave him a gentle kiss on the lips. 'That, my prince, is for good luck.' She grinned and made her way towards the door.

Bernard's face was crimson, but he stood, attempting to make light of the situation. 'How many times do I have to tell you people? I'm the king now.' He laughed as the blush began to dissipate from his cheeks. 'Let's go and address the men.'

He took her hand, and they left the meeting chamber together, both anticipating an end to this horrible chapter in their kingdoms' histories.

~~~~

Cassandra excused herself from the preparations happening within the fortress and took off to her chambers. She had important work of her own to do.

When she was alone, she sat on the edge of her bed and produced her Glimmer from within the folds of her outfit. She held it tight and closed her eyes.

At once, a deep blue glow illuminated the room, filling every corner. She opened her eyes and was not surprised to find herself transported from her chambers, into the altar room of the Glimm. Her personal guide was there to greet her. She had come to think of him as just that, her personal guide, although she was never sure if it was the same man as they all looked so alike. Whoever it was, he was always happy to see her.

'Hello, my queen,' his usual greeting. 'Have you returned for further instruction?'

'Yes. I need to know how I use the powers of the Glimm to command the animals I hold in my thrall. I have tried it so many times, and it always seems to be hit and miss. I also need to know what other powers this Glimmer holds.'

The man smiled at her the way a father might smile at a child learning a new skill. 'My queen, you are holding almost unlimited power. The power of the Glimm guides your hands and your head. Whatever you ask of it, it will do. We do feel the need to advise caution when making your decisions. We urge you to use morality as your compass and motivation. Whatever action the Glimmer performs, be it for good or for ill, there will be consequences. You must be ready for those consequences.'

She nodded and looked at the glowing ball in her hand. 'Can you tell me of the other Glimmer? Was it used to destroy Carnelia in my name?' she asked.

The guide frowned as he looked slowly towards the dusty floor of the great room.

It was all the answer she required.

Anger flared within her, and suddenly she could feel hate and revulsion at the blue orb. 'Do you not control what can and cannot be done with these things?' she hissed through gritted teeth.

The guide, still looking at the floor, intentionally avoiding eye contact with her, shook his head again slowly. His long white hair and beard swung from side to side. 'Unfortunately not. Only the Great Lord Glimm himself holds the power to control a person's actions. If a custodian has become proficient in the use of the Glimmer, all we can offer is guidance. To attempt to coerce the use for good. If someone is Koll-Nor bent on destruction ...' he looked at her, his eyes blazing with the blue reflection but his facial features still sad, '...there is little we can do about it.'

Cassandra stared at the glowing ball. She sighed deeply and held it tighter in her grip. 'I still can't grasp even the basic uses of it. How am I supposed to defeat someone who has had years of use, and knows its secrets so well?'

'That is why you practice, my lady. You're right that the other custodian has held her Glimmer for longer than you, but bitterness and spite have grown in tandem with her skills. Even though she seems to have mastered it, believe me, she has barely scratched the surface of what they can do. In you, my order has belief. The Glimm see the skills that are within you.' He paused for a moment, and Cassandra was sure that his eyes burned an even deeper blue than before. 'You, my child, have a totem.'

'A what?' she asked, cocking her head.

The guide smiled. It was a sly smile, but not a nasty one. It was filled with guile and mischief, making him look younger than he seemed. 'A totem! It is a kind of spirit guide. I look to you, and I see …' he considered her for a few, rather uncomfortable, moments. It felt as if he were looking through her, inside her somehow. 'I see a blue butterfly,' he continued. 'This is your totem, and you must use it to its full extent.'

Cassandra tried to contain the smile she could feel growing at the side of her lips. 'Is it akin to Endellion's fireflies?'

The man's smile faded, and he leaned into her. She thought he was going to put his hand on her shoulder before she remembered they could not touch. 'It is and it isn't. They are monstrous things, mutations. The firefly is a strong totem, but why she would pervert them as she does, I do not know. But come now, we've talked far too long. Now is the time that you must practice. What do you wish to do?'

'I want to learn the ways of the Glimm. I wish to become a master and bring the old ways back …'

The guide raised his hands to stop her in her tirade. Although there was still a smile hiding beneath his beard, the rest of his face looked pained. 'Ah, stop now, my child. I believe I have confused you with talk of you being able to do anything. There is one constant that cannot be altered, not even by a Glimm. That constant is time itself. The old ways of the Glimm are gone, *never* to be returned. We had our days, and the old ways are no longer the ways of this world. The consequences of bringing them back would be dire indeed. The world has moved on.'

'Always with the consequences,' she smiled.

He smiled back, and the levity that had been missing in his face returned. 'Consequences can teach us many things. If we act without heed to the consequences, then what is the point of acting at all?'

Cassandra thought she had just been given a modicum of advice, *good advice too!*

'Now, my child, we must practice. I want to see the rise of the butterfly within you.'

4.

ALEXANDER WAS PROWLING the busy courtyard, searching the nooks and crannies and the dark door-stoops. He couldn't get the old woman who woke him from his slumbers out of his mind. He knew he had seen her somewhere before, and he needed to know if she had called him brother or if it had been a trick of his sleepy brain.

'What are you doing, my brother?'

On hearing himself being referred to as *my brother*, he snapped around towards the voice. He was disappointed to see his sister addressing him. 'Oh, nothing,' he replied, 'I was just looking for someone I met recently.'

Cassandra pulled a bemused face and laughed. 'Oh yeah? A girl, perhaps?'

He blushed deeply at the chiding. 'No, stupid. It was a woman.'

'Please don't tell me you have fallen in love with a chamber crone twice your age?' she kidded him, rousing a laugh from the guardsmen who were mounted, ready for the long ride.

He blushed and flashed his sister an angry glare. 'No, Cass. You sent her to me earlier to wake me for the ride. I have the strangest feeling I know her from somewhere, but I cannot put my finger on it. I think I saw her in Azuria before the war, but I can't seem to remember.'

'Put it out of your head, my brave knight. We have a long ride ahead of us.'

Alexander felt himself deflate. 'You're right. It's just that, I'm thinking I met her in Azuria, and I'm wondering how she could have gotten herself here, to Outpost Two?'

'I said to put it out of your mind, brother. Now, let's ride!'

A cheer rose through the encampment as Endellion reared her horse. She whipped it on the backside and galloped out through the opened gate. She was followed closely by Alexander and one hundred and fifty riders.

~~~~~

A few hours into the ride and Alexander was ahead of the witch who he saw as his sister. She was watching him, noticing the handling of his steed was rather erratic. She could see he was troubled by her mistake this morning. She pulled alongside him.

'Alex,' she whispered. 'Do you fancy a little bit of adventure?'

'I–I'm not sure, my sister. The last time we had an…'

'Oh, don't be afraid, Alex. It won't be like last time,' she assured him. 'We're due a stop soon to water the horses, and ourselves. When we do, I need you to meet me, away from everyone else. We're going to have ourselves a little bit of fun.'

'OK, my queen,' he replied with an unenthusiastic smile.

~~~~

Within the hour, they were stopped at a scheduled waterhole and had set up a makeshift camp, complete with fires and grills to cook their food. Alexander was in a far corner of the camp, sitting alone with his plate filled with beans and jerked beef. All he was doing was pushing the food around the plate. His appetite had gone. It had fled the moment his sister asked him if he'd wanted an adventure.

His heart fell into the pit of his stomach when he saw her walking out of camp accompanied by two soldiers. He watched them disappear behind the back of a makeshift tent.

His meal was over.

He didn't have the stomach for it anyway. He made his way to the waterhole to wash his plate in the large tank that had been drawn for this purpose. He spied Cass again. This time she was walking towards the horses. She was with another soldier, but he couldn't tell if it was one of the same men as before. He wiped his dish and made to follow her.

The horses were tethered together, eating from a trough of oats and hay, with another trough filled with water next to it. The beasts were hungry and thirsty from the long ride and were milling about, vying for access to their refreshments. He lost sight of his sister between the large animals and was almost ready to give up navigating between them when he felt a tapping on his shoulder.

He turned to see his sister standing behind him with a beaming smile on her face. *How did she get behind me?* he thought.

'Hey, Alex,' she whispered. 'Let's go and have that adventure, eh?' she finished before running away from him, playfully.

He liked the way she was smiling. It brought happy memories of back home in Azuria, when they would run and play for hours and hours, before their mother died and she became queen and became so serious all the time. He ran after her. Suddenly the smell of the horses and the sense of the promised adventure before him didn't seem so daunting.

They ran out of camp, towards a large copse of trees.

~~~~

A while later, the riders were mounted on their horses. The make-shift troughs, tents, stoves, and tables had been washed, dismantled, packed, and stored. Shout of 'Let's ride' rose from the front of camp, and a few horses reared onto their mighty back legs. A cheer ripped through the company as they galloped away from the waterhole.

Queen Cassandra and her brother at the forefront of the pack.

5.

IT WAS A single blue butterfly.

It wasn't an overly impressive specimen.

Its thin wings were pale with a sickly blue spreading out in waves from the centre. It spread from the lightest pale blue through to a kind of royal blue.

It was almost the colour of Azuria.

The sickly-looking thing fluttered around the altar room, and around the heads of the Glimm present, who were watching the phenomenon with delight.

Cassandra's guide, whichever one it was, was overjoyed, with a smile spread across his face. She thought if he smiled any further, he was at risk of the top of his head falling off.

'You have worked wonders today, child. You came with rudimentary thrall skills, and now you have created your own totem.

Never have we seen such control in such a short space of time. It would seem you are a natural,'

Cassandra was overwhelmed. Whatever she wanted the butterfly to do, all she had to do was think it, and the insect would do it. It would swirl if she asked it to, it would land if she asked it to, even on her hand.

'Remember, this is an extension of your personality. Do not hesitate to use it however you must. If you need to sacrifice it, then remember it only lives because you commanded it to do so. If it needs to die to serve your purpose, then you must not hesitate to allow it. Love it if you want, but know what it is. It is in your thrall, it will do your bidding, whatever that might be.'

She was listening and nodding. 'I'll remember, although I don't know of any situation where I would be required to kill a butterfly,' she laughed.

Her Glimm guide smiled too. 'You never know what will happen, my child.'

'Can I take this back into my world, the real world, I mean?'

'Yes, you can. But you may require further practice before you do. Controlling one here is excellent work for one day. Controlling one hundred, or one thousand, or even one hundred thousand in your real world? That, my child, is a different matter.'

She watched as the butterfly fluttered down, landing on her hand. As it rested its wings, Cassandra sighed.

'I think you should rest now. You have done well today, taken your first steps into the mystical world of the Glimmer. We should resume this another day.'

'Yes,' she agreed, 'I think I should go. I'll probably be needed elsewhere this night. Thank you for your help.' She offered these thanks not only to her guide but to all the Glimm who were present.

She opened her eyes and was instantly in her chambers.

Hiding the Glimmer back in the folds of her gown, she hurried to the door. Herself and Bernard had made the decision to not let anyone know about the Glimmer, at least until she had more of an understanding and control of it. With the naming of Endellion as a witch and all the talk of black magic and dark rain helping to overrun Carnelia so quickly, it would be prudent not to let them know that she was in possession of the same magic. So off she went to the battlements of Outpost Three, with her Glimmer secure in her hidden pocket.

~~~~

As she made her way to the battlements, the morning was still dark, but on the horizon the first shoots of daylight were beginning to grow from over the mountains. The sight of the men she had come to know and to trust around her, The Ferals, dressed in the armour of the Azurian guard, made her feel strangely at home. These men had become brothers to her, and she loved the uniforms they were wearing.

Bernard approached her. She took a moment to look at him, to marvel at the man he had become in the short time they had gotten to know each other. When first they had met, when she had been dragged into the camp as a prisoner, he had been young, arrogant, and childish. Now, the man before her was anything but. He was a leader, and he had gained the trust and, more importantly, the respect of every man under his command. Not only because he had been their prince but because he was now their commander. Cassandra had fallen in love with the King of Carnelia. *What would my mother think?* she thought with a wry smile.

'What are you smirking at, my lady?' Bernard asked with humour.

'Oh, nothing. I'm just having a moment, thinking about how far we've come.'

Bernard nodded as he regarded the oncoming daylight. 'Where have you been? Ambric will be here soon, and I need to address the men. I need you to let them know what's happening within Azuria and who is leading their kingdom.' As he spoke, he gestured towards the group of two hundred or so men who were huddled against the far wall of the courtyard. They had been stripped of their outer armour and were dressed in civilian clothing.

'What am I to tell them? They already mistrust me due to our deception. Do you think any of them are going to trust me now?'

Bernard shrugged. 'In truth? I don't know. But if we don't try, it will be an opportunity lost. The more we bring over to our cause, the better. The Ferals are only made up of three hundred or so men and women, the Rebels are only slightly larger. It gives us a little more than one thousand soldiers. What good is that against a whole kingdom? We'll have no chance if battle comes.'

Cassandra sighed and shook her head. She looked at the men, the Azurians. *They are* my *people,* she thought. *They must hear my words if I'm to save them, to bring them back from the brink that Endellion has taken them to.* 'I'll see what I can do,' she said with a sigh. 'How long do we have before Ambric is here?'

'He should be here within the hour. He'll want me to release these prisoners to him. He has a stronghold within the woods where he'll likely imprison them. I think we have a good chance of turning some of them.'

She looked at the shivering men, all of them shackled and all of them cold and frightened. She agreed with Bernard. Some of them, on seeing the face of their real queen, may come over to their aid. Either way, she knew she had to try. They were her kin. 'Very well. If you think it will help and keep some of them from imprisonment, then what harm could it do?'

Where the men were standing, there was a make-shift stage where the Feral guard kept watch over the prisoners. As Cass climbed onto it, the prisoners looked up at her. Each face was filled with hate, and there were shouts, most of them unsavoury, aimed her way. Ignoring them, she waited for calm.

'All of you. Look at me and listen.'

The glares felt like a physical force bearing down on her, oppressing her. She considered walking off the stage, giving it up as a bad job, thinking they were never going to listen to a teenager like her. But one look back towards Bernard, seeing him tip his head towards her, gave her all the encouragement she needed. She steeled herself, gritted her teeth, and turned back towards the men. She stared at them. She could feel empathy for the betrayal, deceit, and hatred they had for her. She was supposed to be their queen, their champion in the war against Carnelia, their leader; but here she was now, their captor.

She swallowed hard, wondering how to start this address. She rubbed her greasy hands over her tunic and scanned her audience.

'I know you all must be thinking the worst of me right now, and you have every right to do so. You must be thinking that I'm a turn coat queen. That I have deserted my post and now run wild with these Ferals. But I implore you to listen to what I have to say. I'm here to tell you the truth. It may be difficult for you to hear, to understand, but with every fibre of my being, I promise you it is the truth.' She took a moment to swallow again. It was difficult as her mouth was almost dry. She wished she had brought some water on the stage with her.

'I am the Queen of Azuria.'

This caused a mumble of consternation from the crowd, and Cassandra turned towards Bernard. Her brow ruffled. She felt she was losing the crowd. With another nod of his head, he urged her on. She cleared her throat and continued.

'I am Queen Cassandra, but I'm not the same Queen Cassandra who has been leading you all on a merry dance this last year. I am not the Queen Cassandra who ordered a war against the Kingdom of Carnelia.'

This statement caused a return of the mumblings from the Azurian men. 'Well, you certainly look like her, you witch,' came a shout from the back of the group. The spiteful laughter this caused was infectious, and it spread through the men like wildfire. A few of the Ferals advanced on the crowd to stop them laughing, their weapons raised, ready to strike with the hilts of their swords.

Cassandra raised her hands to stop them. 'Yes,' she shouted over the shouts and laughs. 'You're right, I do look very much like her, don't I? But ask yourself this. If I *was* her, then why would I be here with these Ferals, sleeping rough in the forest, not bathing, and stinking like a wild animal? Why would I not be enjoying the spoils of my war in my comfortable chambers, in my very own castle?'

She watched as some faces in the crowd stopped jeering and listened. There were still too many ruffled brows and narrow eyes for her liking, but there were a few who looked open to what she was saying.

'It's because you have been duped!' This was a bold statement, and it caused more of the critics in the crowd to stop jeering her for a moment while they listened to what she had to say. Buoyed by the shift in temperament, she continued. 'This hasn't been your fault. You have been tricked by a witch whose name is Endellion. She has powers, and one of them is the ability to look like me. I do not know how she is able to perform this,' she lied. 'But she can. She is to blame for the attacks on Carnelia.'

'This is a great story for naughty children who won't sleep, but tell me, can you prove any of it?' came another shout—it might have even been the same person.

This was where her argument stalled. She sighed and her shoulders dropped, she suddenly felt more alone up on this stage than she had moments earlier. The pause made her uncomfortable, it also made her audience shift and murmur.

'Sadly, I don't have any way of proving this to you.'

This truth was met with a chorus of boos and hisses.

Then, a thought occurred to her. There was an angle she could take on this, one that might swing more than a few of them in her favour.

'Are any of you men familiar in the ways of the Glimm?' she asked. It was a question they obviously had not been expecting as it silenced the majority almost instantly. They began to look to each other questioningly.

'The ways of the Glimm,' she repeated. She knew from her upbringing that the ways of the Glimm were well known but seldom practiced. As a religion, it was on the fringes of being ignored completely. 'I'm like you. I never really had time for religion, there were too many rules and regulations, and I never gave much mind.'

There were more mumblings from the crowd as they wondered where this was going. They weren't the only ones. Bernard and his Ferals were wondering too.

Well, if ever there's a time to reveal something, it must be now, she thought, reaching into her pocket and caressing the Glimmer inside. For a moment, she hesitated. *I've just been talking about Endellion being a*

119

witch, and now I'm about to show them something that could label me as the same. She breathed deep and pulled the orb from her gown. She looked at it before holding it up for the crowd to see. As she did, she closed her eyes and the Glimmer shone.

A deep blue glow emanated from her hands, casting its light over her and the crowd before her. There was a complete silence.

'This is a Glimmer,' she shouted. 'There are two of these in the world. One is blue, the other red. Many thousands of years ago, a dying religion gave these as gifts to the two largest tribes in the land. One was given to the tribe that eventually became Carnelia, and the other to Azuria. These orbs are the source of our nations' names. They have been lost for many years, kept in secret locations beneath the castle of each kingdom.'

She paused to take in the impact of what she was telling the men. The interested faces in the crowd outnumbered the disinterested ones by at least two to one. She was happy with the way it was turning. She looked at Bernard again and grinned as she watched him shake his head.

'My brother, Alexander, gave this to me as a good luck talisman on the morning I left Azuria to meet with the Carnelians, after the death of my mother. He was late, and he sprinted through the courtyard to catch me. He was panting, out of breath as he handed it to me. He told me he found it in an old room somewhere beneath the castle. Many Azurians had begged me not to take that trip, many told me it was a folly, but none protested as much as he.' She wiped a tear from her eye as she spoke of Alexander. 'But I had to go. I had to see why they had shunned us. That was the last time I had any contact with him.' She bowed her head. She didn't want to relay this last bit of information, but she knew she must. 'It wasn't, however, the last time I saw him. On the day Carnelia fell, I watched with horror and dread as my brother rode out of the city gates. He was holding an Azurian victory banner and was riding alongside the witch Endellion. The very one you call your queen.'

'I remember that,' a voice shouted from the crowd, and she looked down to see a familiar face. It was one of her guards, one who had not been selected for the mission to Carnelia. 'I remember the day you left. I was in the courtyard, and I watched your brother hand you something. I also remember him being upset for your leaving.' The guard stepped forward; he never took his eyes from Cassandra's face the whole time. 'I saw it was a glowing blue ball, similar, if not the same as the one you hold now. I have seen another like it, but it glows red. I've seen it in the possession of the que—' He paused for a moment, rethinking his words. 'The woman who resembles our queen, in Azuria.' He turned towards his fellow soldiers and shouted. All of them shifted their gaze from Cassandra to him. 'I believe her. I believe this could be the true queen. If not, how could she have known the things she spoke of?' He turned back towards Cassandra and dropped to his knee, bowing his head. 'My queen, I am a simple man, but I believe what you say. I beg your forgiveness for blindly following an imposter.'

There were more boos and hisses coming from the crowd as he dropped, but they were fewer than before.

The majority stayed silent.

121

~~~~

'It's working.' Bernard whispered as he listened to her speech. 'I can't believe it. It's truly working.'

The Feral next to him was smiling, shaking his head. 'Never underestimate the power of true royalty …'

Bernard snapped his head towards him, his eyes were narrowed. 'What's that supposed to mean?' His smile quickly became a laugh.

The Feral, Matthew, one of his oldest friends, laughed as he grabbed Bernard's shoulder. He held it with a friendly but powerful grip before pushing him away, still laughing.

6.

'I SEE THEM. They're coming …' came the cry from the top of the wall.

'How far off?' was the reply.

'I'd estimate ten miles. Maybe less.'

Bernard heard the shout and looked to Robert Ambric, who was standing next to him within the courtyard of Outpost Three. He and a troupe of his Rebels had arrived less than an hour earlier and were preparing to move the remaining prisoners before Endellion and her riders arrived. 'I think you must work in haste, Ambric.'

'I will, lad,' he replied, still looking up at the guard who had made the shout. 'I'm thankful to Cassandra for lessening my burden. She managed to bring over half of them into the fold.'

Bernard nodded, and his mouth pulled down into a leer, albeit a proud one. 'Oh, it was a rousing speech, sir. If only you could have heard it.'

Ambric nodded. 'Right, I'll be off then. We have a den nearby that can hold up to three hundred men comfortably, to a fashion. When her riders yield, send message, and I'll come back for them.' With that, he grabbed Bernard by the arm in a tight grip and shook it vigorously. 'You're a good soldier, Bernard. I hope one day I'll get to call you king.'

Bernard gripped the arm back. 'I don't think I could ever not call you *sir*, Sir Ambric. You have mentored me well. But enough sentiment, you best be off. You need to get mileage between your party and here before the fly falls into our web. Glimm speed to you, Sir Ambric.'

'And good luck to you and yours, Bernard.' With that, he commanded his men to ready themselves to move out. He mounted his own horse and was off. The Rebels followed, dragging the manacled prisoners of the Azurian outpost with them.

7.

'MAYBE FIVE MILES out now, sir!'

'OK, positions, everybody,' Bernard ordered. 'This must look like a normal Azurian encampment.' Every man within the fortress had been outfitted in the armour of Azuria, and each had a thin red line down the sides of their bodies to differentiate them from the real Azurians if it did come to battle. 'Do we have confirmation that Endellion is within their numbers?'

There was a moment's pause, then the reply. 'They're too far out for positive identification, but I can confirm there is a lady in the entourage, and what appears to be a young boy also.'

Cassandra's heart leaped at this news. 'No matter how hard he fights, Alexander is not to be harmed,' she ordered. 'He's only a boy who's had his head turned for over a year by a witch.' She hated calling Endellion a witch because if she truly was one, then she herself must be too. But the term was a necessary means to her end. Everyone agreed that the boy would not be harmed. He would be subdued but not harmed.

The atmosphere within the castle walls was tense. The silence only broken every now and then by the odd cough or rattle of weapons as they waited anxiously for the knock on the portcullis and the shout for permission to enter.

Cassandra was gazing at her surroundings. The men fascinated her. Each one had their own story to tell, a story that was written on their faces. She felt for each of them. They had been thrown into this chaotic life, just as she had. They had no other course of action, just like her. When Endellion was secure in her custody later that afternoon, stripped of her Glimmer and her firefly army, she would have a lot of explaining to do.

Amidst the sorrow and empathy she felt for her companions, the seeds of excitement were also growing. The dichotomy of these conflicting feelings was not lost on her. She was looking forward to seeing Alexander. He was such a sweet boy, and she hoped Endellion hadn't soured him against the world too much. She hoped that his good-natured heart was still beating and hadn't been replaced by a black hole!

'Two miles and closing.' The shout from the walls snapped her out of her thoughts, and she felt the beginnings of butterflies, fluttering and dancing away in the pit of her stomach. 'I can confirm that Cassandra, or whoever it is imitating her, is indeed within the vanguard. She is surrounded by roughly a hundred men ...' the man on the walls paused for a moment; Cass's heart was beating rapidly in her throat. 'Yes, I can confirm that the fifteen men in the advanced vanguard does include her young brother.'

'How does he look?' Cassandra couldn't help but shout out to the guards. 'Does he look healthy?'

Once again there was a pause from the man on the walls as he looked out of the fortress, towards the advancing party. 'From here, ma'am, he looks fit and well.' The man smiled down at her, his face kindly. 'I'll tell you this too, he can handle a horse for a boy of his age,' he added.

Cassandra smiled. It was a bitter-sweet smile, filled with memories and loss. *He was always scared of the horses ... he must have been practicing.*

~~~~

Within minutes of the shout, there was a loud bang on the portcullis. It echoed around the castle courtyard. Everyone within the walls was quiet, looking to one another for reassurance. Bernard was slapping his hands on the shoulders of as many of his men as he could, encouraging them to go about their business as normal, desperate not to cause any undue alarm or suspicion.

'Permission to enter the encampment,' came the stern shout from beyond the wall.

'By whose authority?' came the steady reply from one of Bernard's men, standing behind the door. There were several men to either side of him, each one ready to pincer the Azurian guard the moment they entered the courtyard. They all wanted as little bloodshed as possible.

'By the order of Queen Cassandra of Azuria, her brother Prince Alexander, and all her brave riders. Now raise these gates and let us in.'

The men on the walls looked down towards Bernard and nodded their confirmation that it was indeed Endellion and her riding party. Bernard nodded back, giving his permission to open the gates, and welcome their guests inside.

~~~~

The men who made up The Ferals, who less than a year ago were mostly just boys playing at being soldiers, were going about their business as usual within the compound walls. Although focused on their mission, none could resist the urge to watch as the gate lifted. The metal rattled and squealed in its hinges as it was pulled up to herald the arrival of Queen Cassandra of Azuria—or rather, Endellion, witch of nowhere, presider over the destruction of the Carnelian nation.

As the first riders entered the fortress, the men dressed in the uniform of Azuria attended to them and their steeds. Bernard had positioned them around the perimeter of the castle in the guise of performing manual labours. He had lined men up in the centre of the courtyards in the guise of a military tattoo in honour of the queen. All were sporting the uniform of Azuria, albeit with a thin red line painted down the side of it.

None of the new arrivals noticed the change in personnel.

Bernard was stood to attention before the tattoo. His face was stoic, but his eyes were darting back and forth among the new arrivals, searching for a sign of the witch.

Cassandra was busying herself in a corner, blending into the background as best she could. She was also studying the newcomers, searching for Endellion, and for her brother too.

Eventually, she was rewarded but still needed to double take, as her mirror image, mounted upon a white steed, trotted into the courtyard, walking into their trap. She was surrounded by her guards, each alert and ready to spring into action at any given moment. Then she saw her brother, and her heart broke. It was beating in her mouth, and if she hadn't been so nervous, she thought there would have been tears welling in her eyes. She noticed that he had grown in their year apart, he was now so tall.

With another squeal, the rusted metal of the heavy gate came crashing down. The newly arrived Azurian guard turned, searching for the source of the sound.

There was a momentary look of shock, followed by confusion when they realised they were now locked within the courtyard of their own fortress.

A shout roared from somewhere within the throng of men, taking the Azurian riders by surprise.

'Now! Ferals, take them.'

Bernard yelled his order at the top of his lungs. The military tattoo that had been set up to welcome Queen Cassandra into Outpost Three broke apart instantly. All the men with the thin red lines down the sides of their uniforms unsheathed their broadswords, and the men on the walls turned inwards, bringing forth their loaded crossbows. Each weapon trained on the Royal Guard.

The riders did not know what was happening. They had been taken completely by surprise. Some reared their mounts but were quickly subdued by the Ferals within the courtyard. Other than this, there was very little resistance as they knew they had been successfully ambushed.

'Queen Cassandra, Prince Alexander, present yourselves as prisoners of The Ferals of Azuria,' Bernard shouted as he stepped forward towards the white horse that Endellion was mounted upon.

Queen Cassandra silently dismounted her steed. Every weapon was trained on her and her men. She fixed her clothing and strode to where Bernard was stood. Her head hung low, and there was an air of defeat about her. With a petrified look in his eyes, Alexander, too, dismounted his steed and followed her.

The activity in the centre of the courtyard had the attention of every man in the castle, Azurian guard and Feral alike.

Bernard looked at the woman who was the doppelgänger of Queen Cassandra in every way he could see. They were the same height, had the same hair colour, the same deep blue eyes. *Remarkable,* he thought as she trudged towards him.

He shook his head as she stopped before the crowd, his prisoner. *At last, we can end this ...* 'Endellion,' he shouted loud enough for everyone to hear what he had to say. 'You are hereby charged with treason, witchcraft, and heresy. You have impersonated royalty, taken control of the great nation of Azuria, and with your dark arts, destroyed the great and noble nation of Carnelia. How do you plead to these charges?'

Endellion said nothing; she just stared at him. Her beautiful face devoid of emotion. Her eyes stared blankly.

~~~~

The real Cassandra made her way to where Bernard and the witch were staring at each other. An audible gasp tore through the fortress as each of them, guard and Feral alike, gawped at what they were witnessing.

Cassandra's gaze fell upon Endellion. She studied her face. *I know I've seen her before, looking like me, but it is still horrible,* she thought. 'Endellion,' she shouted, again loud enough to be heard in every corner of the crowded courtyard. 'I can't say I know who you are or what your motivations are, but I now demand you yield in the names of the two great nations of Carnelia, and Azuria.'

Both prisoners looked at Bernard and Cassandra. They were still silent, their faces looking as if they had been carved in stone. Even in the light of the accusations against them, the suffering she had inflicted on the people of Carnelia, the atrocities that had been done that day—family members savaging family members, biting, punching, kicking each other to death in the streets—still, the woman and her brother showed no emotions.

It caused Bernard's anger to boil, and he could not help himself; he reached out and grabbed Endellion by her riding shirt and forced her onto the floor, to kneel before him. This she did with no resistance whatsoever. He drew his long sword and addressed the crowd before him. 'I want everyone present to witness and to know that I hold no pleasure whatsoever in the taking of another's life, be it in battle or otherwise. But this woman ... I feel she should not be allowed to continue. Her inhumane crimes against Carnelia and against Azuria are second only to her crimes against nature. I do this today to address the balance, and to attempt to bring harmony between our two nations.' He spared a fleeting glance at the witch kneeling before him and noted she and her brother were still staring emotionless ahead of them. Their eyes glazed and focused on nothing. Putting it down to fear of the situation they found themselves in, he continued to address the men and the Azurian Guards. 'I need you to bear witness to what happens here now. Take this with you, share it with your countrymen. Tell them of the witch Endellion, but most of all, keep this in in your head and in your hearts.'

He looked towards Cassandra. His face was solemn. He whispered, 'Cass, I'm so sorry, but this has to be done ...'

She closed her eyes and nodded. As she opened them again, they were drawn to her brother, to Alexander. He had not given her any acknowledgement since they had entered the encampment. He seemed not to have noticed her at all. She couldn't believe her own sweet brother could have been so corrupted by this scheming, horrible, murderous woman. She nodded, attempting to get his attention, but the boy ignored her, as if he had never seen her before in his life. *He'll know me soon enough,* she thought, *when that woman's head leaves her shoulders and she reverts to her natural state.*

With his broad sword in his hand, Bernard pulled back Endellion's hair. He raised his foot and put it on the witch's shoulder, pushing her down onto the floor and holding her there. 'Do you have any last words, witch?' he asked loud enough that everyone in the courtyard would be able to hear. When the woman didn't react to this question, he shrugged. 'So be it. With the powers vested in me as leader of The Ferals, and with the royal blood of Carnelia flowing through my veins, I sentence you to death for treason and regicide.' With one good swing, the cut was true. The witch's head was severed clean off her body.

The blood from the wound flowed in a tide of crimson. Both Bernard and Cassandra were caught in its spatter, as was the prince. The boy wiped the red liquid from his eyes as Bernard leant down and picked up the head, which lay next to the crumpled body. He lifted it up towards him men before making a show of it towards the Azurian Royal Guard. He wanted everyone to see what had become of their *queen.*

'This is the head of a traitorous witch,' he shouted. 'She is not your queen.'

The silence in the courtyard was physical. Every eye was on either the bloodied prince holding up the severed head or the body of the dismembered queen laid out in her blue Azurian riding armour.

He was expecting more than the silence he was witnessing. He thrust the head up higher for everyone to see, anticipating a roar or applause or … something other than the complete silence of the fort.

Something strange had happened. Even though it was something he and Cassandra were expecting, the feel of the head changing in his hands had been strange and unnatural. It felt like a snake slithering through his fingers. His first impulse was to drop it and pull his hands as far away from it as possible, but he knew in doing so, he would lose respect, not only from his men, but from the prisoners too. He looked at the head as the colour of the hair began to change. He watched it lighten. It was an odd spectacle to witness features move on the dead face, but that is what they did.

The silence from the crowd continued as everyone observed what was happening. The face's feminine features shifted and became rugged. As the thick hair Bernard was holding began to recede, he lost his grip on it. He dropped his dripping sword and grabbed at the head before it fell to the ground. As he brought it up to eye level, he was horrified …

The face was indeed no longer Cassandra's, but it wasn't Endellion's either. It had changed into that of an older man. His fat, stubbled jowls were smeared with blood, and his narrow, crow's-feet lined eyes were closed. With dawning horror, Bernard looked at the face, then he looked down towards the body lying on the ground. That, too, had changed. It was no longer the thin, youthful body of the Queen of Azuria but was now the body of a short, stout Azurian guard.

Bernard yelped and stepped backwards. He slipped on blood, causing him to drop the offending head onto the floor. It began to roll towards where Alexander was kneeling, still wearing the same expressionless face.

Without flinching, the boy picked the head up from the floor and looked at it. Cassandra held her breath. She was distraught that her little brother had witnessed this, especially at his tender, and impressionable age. But then she was also glad that he had seen the work of Endellion personally. Maybe it would give him the clarity he needed to see through what the witch had been telling him, whispering to him.

As these thoughts flashed through her head, Alexander began to change too. His face grew long and thin, and a thick beard grew in rapid speed. It covered his chin and cheeks. His hair grew at the back but receded at the front, and it changed to a dirty, greasy lighter shade. His face contorted, changing from her sweet twelve-year-old brother to an ugly, battle scarred, and world weary fifty-year-old guardsman.

Cassandra gasped as she gazed on what her own flesh and blood had just become. She, too, took a step back, holding on to Bernard's arm for support.

'What the …' he whispered as the man who had been Prince Alexander mere seconds ago looked around him, bewildered as to where he was, and why he was there!

8.

JUST UNDER A mile from where the queen's riders had encamped before they marched into their trap, Alexander and Endellion—in the guise of Cassandra—were hiding, tucked well out of sight within a copse of bushes. They had watched the proceedings from this vantage as their riders had ridden off without them. She had been sly enough not to shield Alexander from seeing the two men disguised as them at the head of the army.

'Why did we not ride with the protection of our Royal Guard?' he asked. 'They are one hundred and fifty strong. We're now only two. Surely it would make sense to stay with them. Safety in numbers.'

Endellion turned away from the passing men on horseback and looked at her pretend brother. She smiled kindly as she reached out and stroked his dark, blue-tinged hair. 'Because, my inquisitive brother, who is easier to see? A band of one hundred and fifty men on horseback, galloping at speed, kicking up plumes of dust, while dragging tents, cooking utensils, and whatever else? Or two pedestrians, out of sight and able to duck into bushes and trees at any given moment, to hide themselves?'

'Well,' he nodded, 'if you put it that way, then I see why we are not with them,' he replied, but his face was still masked with confusion and questions.

'All we needed to do is keep our heads down and ourselves hidden while they march.'

'For what reason?' he asked.

'Because Outpost Three is a trap. I conversed with the fireflies when we were in Outpost Two. I sent them forth as reconnaissance. I didn't like the feeling I was getting from some of the men in our guard. I feared treachery was afoot. They reported back to me that something was happening at Outpost Three, something that would not be good for us, brother. We must keep our wits about us. I'm not sure who we can trust, other than each other, that is.' She looked deep into his eyes, staring intensely at him. 'My brother, you do trust me, don't you?'

His eyes opened wide, and she was more than happy to read the fear he was feeling, reflecting in his features. He nodded curtly before answering.

'I'm your brother and your knight. I'll be at your side until the day we die.'

'So, I can trust you, can't I?'

'Yes,' he answered. She loved the confusion in the youngster's eyes. 'That goes without saying. Why do you ask me these questions?'

'Because, my brother, there is work ahead of us that has to be done. I need to know that no matter what you see, or what people tell you they have seen, you are my brother and I am your sister. We are all we have, the only ones we can truly trust.' She smiled and looked up into the sky. 'Well, us and …'

She heard them before she could see them. She could feel the heavy throb of the beating of their wings in her chest. A swarm of fireflies descended from the sky; hundreds of them. She watched as Alexander's hair was blown back from his head on their approach. A joyous smile spread across her face as she enjoyed the feel of their multiple wings buzzing in unison as they hovered above them

She was grinning like a lunatic as her winged army paused, waiting for her command. She spared a glance at Alexander. The awe on his face for these reverent beasts was evident for her to see. *I have him wrapped around my little finger,* she thought. 'Our fireflies!' she shouted over the drone of their wings.

As if beckoned, the huge insects began to descend on the small copse where she and Alexander hid.

'Quickly, climb onto one and hold tight. They fly fast, but they will not drop you. They offer us the best protection we can get.'

The excited boy did not need to be told twice. As she watched him climb upon the thorax of the nearest firefly, his face was the happiest she had seen it in a long while. The beast curved its body, offering him a seat, and wrapped two of its strong legs around him, holding him tightly and securely.

Endellion climbed onto another and sat in the same manner, secure for their flight. 'We must make haste, young Alex. With luck, we should make it to Carnelia long before our guards do. We will ensure our version of accounts regarding the Royal Guard's treachery is the one they hear first, and the one that they believe. They will not doubt their queen, and when, or if, the guards return, they will be hung for their treason.'

'Why are you so certain they were working with the enemy, Cass?' Alexander asked; there was an innocence in his high-pitched voice.

She knew it was pure! *We will soon rid ourselves of that,* she thought with a small smile. 'I overheard them talking about the Ferals and how they were due to liaise with them between Outpost Two and Three. They were going to hand us over to them, Alex, for gold or who knows what. I heard talk that they no longer needed you, and that your head would make a lovely decoration mounted over the portcullis of Outpost Three. If I hadn't been fortuitous enough to overhear them, you would most likely be dead now, and I would be held captive, raped, and beaten.'

Alexander shook his head. 'Bastards,' he seethed.

'Traitorous bastards,' Endellion replied, her dark heart now singing with the realisation that Alexander was moving over to her side.

'So, will they be looking for us now?' he asked, his hand on the hilt of his sword.

'More likely than not …' she replied.

'Should we hunt them down and kill them, sister? Use our new army?'

Endellion smiled again. *You are going to be such a delightful tool, boy. Now that I have you where I need you.* 'That is a great idea, Alexander. Do you think you could do it, my prince? It would be a bloody pastime.'

The boy grinned a wicked grin, one that Endellion liked very much.

'Yes, let us get some sport. No one sells out the Queen of Azuria. Not on my watch.'

9.

THE THRILL OF the high-speed flight delighted Alexander. The wild wind whipped thorough his hair, pushing his body back into the comfort and safety of his courser, the large flying insect. He tried his best to laugh, to whoop, and scream his way across the sky, but every time he opened his mouth, the wind took his breath away. A few times he panicked a little as he didn't know if he would ever get it back again.

The trees below whizzed past in a way that he could only previously imagine. The powerful beasts were flying at least ten times faster than the fastest horse could run. Their wings buzzed loudly as they flew effortlessly for what seemed like miles.

'There, in those trees,' Endellion shouted over the roar of the onrushing air. 'There's a camp hidden within those trees. I can see it!'

Alexander struggled to see where she was pointing. All he could see for miles were trees, trees, and more trees.

Then he saw it. It was just a small flash of colour in the green.

'Should we check them out? Just to see if they have red-tinged hair?' Endellion laughed, it was a high-pitched scream that Alexander had never heard before, and he gave her a second look. She then pitched her firefly at a steep downward angle towards the trees about a mile away from the camp. Alexander's firefly followed closely behind. He had to grip the legs of the beast to stop himself from falling off. They landed in a small clearing, and the strong legs loosened. He was both relieved and disappointed at the same time.

After they dismounted, Endellion pointed through the trees, and they made their way towards the cooking smells coming from the camp. The fireflies relaxed in the clearing, and the sudden loss of the buzz of their wings felt empty in Alexander's head.

After a while of scrambling through the bushes, they reached a clearing where there were men sitting on watch for the small encampment behind them. He noticed that the men had red-tinged hair.

They were Carnelian.

Endellion turned towards him. 'Shhhh,' she hissed, putting her fingers to her lips.

He scanned the camp and noticed that there were more men dotted around, hidden within the trees.

Smiling, Endellion whispered, 'Brother, you'll need to wait here, and do not move. I'll go and look over that ridge. I want to make sure it's a Ferals camp.'

With that, before he could oppose her decision, she crawled off into the undergrowth and was gone.

~~~~

When she was out of Alexander's sight, she wriggled into a tight crawlspace behind a bush, where she was sure no one could see her. She reached into her pocket and produced her Glimmer. As she closed her eyes, the ball began to glow, and she slowly began to change. Her physical form began to melt as she became less and less human and more insectoid. Before the change was complete, she slipped the Glimmer into a hidden fold within her thorax. Once it was secured, she immersed herself into her new form.

Endellion, in the guise of a firefly, rose from the ground and hovered for a small while, spying on the men who were stationed around the woods. She rose higher and flew nearer to the camp. She could see there were maybe one hundred men camped around a large fire and in the tents behind it. Towards the edge was a group who were shackled together like prisoners. These men all had blue tinged hair. *Azurians*, she thought. *My firefly scouts were right. The Ferals* did *take Outpost Three. These men must be the Rebels. I wonder who is in charge here.*

Then she saw him.

Ambric? she hissed in her head. *How is that possible? He was killed before Carnelia fell.*

She turned, flying back to her original location. Her long, black insect arm reached into the fold in her thorax and touched the Glimmer inside. Instantly, there was a red glow, and she began to change back into

143

Cassandra. She then crawled towards where Alexander was hiding. When she was almost there, she called down her army.

'Alexander,' she whispered. 'It's worse than we imagined. Yes, the men have red tinged hair, that makes them Carnelians, but they are in league with the Azurians.'

Alexander's eyes opened wide at hearing the news. 'What? Do you mean they're traitors?'

'Yes, my brother, traitors. Should we and our firefly army destroy their camp?'

'Yes,' he replied with no hesitation whatsoever.

With a sly smile, she called two of the hovering fireflies down to their position. She climbed on board one of them. 'Saddle up, Alex. Today, we do Azuria a favour.'

With a wild look in his eyes, the youth obliged.

10.

THE MOOD WITHIN the camp was optimistic. The half who were not soldiers, or had not had any official training as soldiers, were being put through their paces by Ambric and a few of his men. Others were going about assigned duties as guardsmen, cooks, or cleaners. Others, who were more adept with weapons, were assigned to hunting and the gathering of wood for the fire. As nobody knew how long they would be encamped in the forest, the officers had suggested they begin to busy themselves making the camp comfortable. Even if they had to move on, they could always come back and use it as a base of operations.

The prisoners were constantly complaining. They could smell the roasting meat of the rabbits and small pigs that were over the fire and the wafts from the bread baking in makeshift ovens made from the clay of the land. They knew all they would be getting would be tasteless oats and clean water.

There was the hustle and bustle of people going about their work, the clanking of swords as men practiced for battle, there was laughing and complaining—in all, it was a functioning camp.

Ambric was attempting to show one of the younger boys, who had been a smithy's apprentice in another life but had shown a keen interest in the ways of combat, how to block an oncoming sword attack from above.

It wasn't going too well.

'No ... no, no. You can't block like that. If you do, the next thrust your opponent makes with be the last one you ever feel. You have left your stomach open to attack. Remember, your opponent won't be looking to stab at you, your armour will protect you from that. What he is looking for is the small chinks in your protection, the bits where the armour creases, where flesh is exposed. You need to do it like this ...' Ambric instructed. He feigned as if he was receiving an attack from an imaginary swordsman coming at him from above. Then he ducked, quick as a flash, and raised his sword to cover his head. At the same time, he raised his armoured forearm to cover his neck from slashes from a downward strike and stop any attack coming at him towards his midriff.

'It looks easy when I do it, I know. I've been training this all my life. These are the fundamentals, boy. They will save you in a fight.' He handed the sword back to the grateful youth, who accepted it with a smile. 'Practice boy, practice ...'

As he walked away, he reached his arms around to support the small of his back, leaned, and grimaced a little. The stretch felt good. With his head tilted towards the sky, he opened his eyes. That was when he noticed something out of the ordinary. There was a deep thrumming noise. It had been in his head for a small while, but he had thought nothing of it, dismissing it, until now.

His gaze swooped the sky backwards and forwards as the realisation of what he was hearing brought visions of his worst, and most recent, nightmares.

A shadow passed over the sun, turning the day dark. All the playful noises of the camp stopped as the shadow passed over them. The low, rhythmic thrum and buzz was all that could be heard in the afternoon air. It wasn't loud enough to assault the ears, but it was low enough for everyone in the camp to feel the vibrations within their bones.

Above them, swarming in a cloud, were hundreds of huge fireflies. The ferocious beasts were hovering in such a way that their stings were pointing towards the ground. Ambric noted that the stout barbs were dripping with a thick, yellow, viscus liquid.

'Men,' he shouted, raising his voice in the way he'd been taught, so that everyone in his vicinity could hear, maybe not the words, but the alert within the shout. 'All of you, present shields. Now! Today, you will learn a real lesson.' He raised his own shield in a defensive position above his head. Most of the men watching him copied. He breathed in deeply, slowing his heartbeat as he had been taught to do in his youth. This gave him the ability to control the levels of adrenaline that would rush through his body, giving him use of them when he needed it most.

147

He prayed to the Glimm that the new recruits had at least listened to, and taken on board, the lessons they had been given.

He knew this otherwise quiet day was about to become a bloodbath.

~~~~~

The attack began!

The deadly flying insects descended on the men below.

They moved slowly at first, and the men looked ready for them. As they flew closer, the archers and the swordsmen took defensive positions. They had heard Ambric's tales of these beasts, even though half of them had taken what he had said with a pinch of salt, as campfire tales. They were all believing him now.

They were ready.

Ambric was ushering the few women and children that had followed them out of Carnelia into cover as he saw the insects' slow descent. 'This isn't right,' he whispered, mostly to himself. He shifted his gaze towards his men and was proud to see them standing ready. Some of the new recruits were laughing. *They think this is going to be easy*, he thought, surprising himself with his anger. He looked up towards the slow-moving insects and realised something about this attack, something everyone else needed to know.

'All of you,' he shouted. 'Cover your heads. This is a decoy.'

As the men turned to see what he was shouting about, the real attack occurred.

From a flank on the left of the first wave, a second wave of fireflies came at them; these came in fast. At least twenty of the aberrations slipped through the gaps of the first wave, stings first. The thick amber poison dripping from the sharp stings was glistening in the sun.

'Get down, now!' Ambric screamed.

But it was already too late. The first wave of diving insects hit, and they hit hard.

He watched as one firefly's sting penetrated the neck of one of the new recruits. As it entered, Ambric watched in slow motion as the blood arched over the attacking beast. The man fell to the ground. There was a sickening crunch that was audible, even over the noise of the attack. It made Ambric flinch, but it also brought him back from the reverie he was currently trapped in. Alert now, he watched as the beast took to the air again with most of the man's body still attached to its sting. A shower of blood and gore dripped from the sky.

Gritting his teeth, Ambric turned to face the battle. His most experienced men had taken the inexperienced ones under their shields. He had time to smile, a wry grin of pride, as he watched the recruits take the given instruction and benefit from it.

One of them was sheltering under the shield of a soldier. With an eager look in his eye, he held his sword in his hand, ready to battle their attackers. Ambric watched as a firefly dived towards an unarmed colleague. At the last possible moment, the recruit darted out from under his cover, slashing at the speeding insect as he moved. He swung his sword in a two-handed slice and caught the firefly across its bloated body. A sickening scream resounded through the air, and a thick squirt of hot yellow poison ejaculated from the monster's belly before it fell in two pieces onto the ground.

Bursting with pride, Ambric watched other heroic enterprises as the battle unfolded around him. His men were holding their own against a mightier and truly terrifying foe. The way these men, his men, fought gave him chills.

Pride always comes just before the fall. This had been one of his mother's favourite sayings, and it rang true to him now as he looked to the skies once more.

A third wave of fireflies came streaming in from the opposite direction of the first two, taking his men completely by surprise. Five of them, including one of his most experienced soldiers, were killed in this attack, impaled on glistening stings while attempting to protect the others from the grasping, powerful legs of the impossible beasts.

To Ambric, it looked like the battle's tide was turning, and not in their favour. He watched helplessly as at least six more men were either taken or killed when, in the confusion of not knowing where the buzzing sounds were coming from, they were simply plucked from the ground.

'What manner of coward controls these monsters?' he growled. 'Show yourself and fight like a real man, if indeed that is what you are.'

Raising his sword and gripping it with both hands, he decided that the battle had lived without him for too long. *If today is the day to die, then so be it*, he thought, relishing his heart beating, no, thumping, in double time. *At least it will be a good death*!

With a piercing cry, he broke cover. As he ran, he saw the recruit he was teaching earlier shielding himself against the great sting of one of the beasts. The boy was doing a heroic job of keeping it away with his shield, but what he couldn't see, and Ambric could, was the second firefly coming at him from behind. Ambric was on it in a flash. With an expert flick of his broadsword, he severed the sting of the attacking insect, and the thing fell to the floor, dying in a pool of its own yellow blood. The grim light from its body was fading.

The recruit thanked him.

'No time for thanks on the battlefield, boy, just keep your wits about you,' he shouted as he ran into another attack.

The fireflies were coming in thick waves, relentless in their task. Ambric could see his men were tiring, and by a quick reckoning, he estimated there were at least twenty of his men decapitated, or worse, on the ground. Even though there were mountains of the beasts lying dead, their numbers were dwindling. His sword passed effortlessly through more of the monstrosities before he stopped to take account of what was happening.

His earlier thought was correct; it was turning into a bloodbath.

'Enough of this,' he shouted over the sounds of battle. 'RETREAT … RETREAT … RETREAT!' he screamed.

Most of the men heard him and got behind his idea straight away, disengaging the enemy and fleeing into the safety of the underground caverns that had been Ambric's reasoning behind the location of the camp.

'Easy to defend and easy to retreat to. The perfect location,' Ambric had said, more than once, when selecting the site.

He'd been here before.

Some of the men had decided that taking on a few more of the fireflies before they retreated might be a good idea. They had been proven wrong. With fewer enemies to target, the beasts wasted no time picking off the easy prey, setting upon them in numbers. They were torn apart, or impaled, within moments. Ambric witnessed it all but couldn't afford time to grieve for any of them; not yet. There was still much to do.

He sheathed his sword and ran for one of the trapdoors to the caverns. Straining, as the hatch hadn't been used in a while, he pulled it open and held it for his retreating men to enter. He braved a look up into the sky and marvelled at the sheer number of advancing insects.

When most of the men who could make it inside had, he began to make his way towards the location of the prisoners. Their screams of fear could be heard over the death throes of his men as they watched the attack happen. It was obvious these men were not in league with their attackers and he could see they were as afraid of them as his own men were.

As he ran towards them, he was roughly pulled back. 'Leave them, Robert.' the soldier shouted at him. 'Save yourself. We need you more that we need them.'

'I can't, they're in my care,' Ambric spat as he shoved the arm from his shoulder. 'I refuse to leave them behind.'

'Look!' the man shouted, pointing towards the sky.

Ambric's eyes followed his indication. Wave after wave of fireflies descended upon the prisoners, tearing them apart, literarily, limb from limb.

As the prisoners were shackled, the poor souls had no possible defence against the formidable, and seemingly relentless foe. Ambric and his colleague watched helplessly as the fireflies ploughed their way through all eighty or so prisoners. The monsters were without mercy and without relent.

With a heavy heart, Ambric averted his eyes from the massacre. He knew the remainder of his men, and the women and children they had acquired along the way, needed him more than the prisoners did now. He made it back to the trapdoor, flanked by two of his men. It confused him to think why the creatures would have been ordered to attack and kill their own men. It made him question who it was controlling them.

Just before he entered the safety of the trapdoor, he spared one more glance towards the shadow of the advancing swarm. He saw something up there; something that turned his blood cold. He narrowed his eyes and wiped the blood and sweat from them, just to make sure that he wasn't seeing things.

He wasn't.

There, at the back of the attack, were two larger insects, larger than all the others. These two were holding back. They looked to be coordinating the battle. Within the grip of the beasts, Ambric could see two people being held in place, riding the beasts like vehicles. He recognised the faces of the two people.

'Cassandra …' he whispered. 'And her brother?'

Ambric and Endellion locked eyes on each other briefly. He watched as twinges of a smile break on her young face. The smile was meant for him. She shouted something toward her brother, something that Ambric couldn't hear, and another wave of fireflies descended towards him.

'Cassandra!' he muttered. *Is it her or the witch?* he thought. *I'd better inform Bernard to be on his toes. He could be letting himself into a trap.* With this confusion running through his head, he made his way through the trapdoor and down into the tunnels.

Eventually, he reached a large cavern that had been manually carved from the hard earth. It was lit with oil lamps. A group of Rebels were waiting inside.

'Is this all that's left?' he asked.

The soldier at the entrance bowed his head. 'I believe it is. We all fought bravely against an insurmountable foe. Those who survived, and those who didn't.'

Ambric put his hand on the soldier's shoulder. 'We will never forget that fact. But right now, we must move quickly to another location. This one has been compromised. Let's regroup and make plans.' He walked away from the rest of the men, down a tunnel, taking a lamp with him as he went. 'I have some things to dwell upon,' he muttered, more to himself than to anyone else.

11.

ENDELLION SAT ASTRIDE her firefly within a small clearing in the forest. She was laughing heartily. Her face was flushed red, and the thin sheen of sweat embracing her brow was glistening in the dying sun. Alexander was also looking flushed. He was sporting a foolish grin, as if he had done something that he knew he shouldn't, but had enjoyed it.

She looked at him, her eyes narrowing like a fox spying the chicken coup before a raid. 'You enjoyed that, didn't you, brother? It was exhilarating, wasn't it?'

Alexander was panting, still trying to catch his breath. All he could do was nod and smile.

'It felt good, didn't it? It's empowering to hold a man's life in your hands. To have the power over if the wretch lives or dies.' She looked at him, the dreamlike glare in his eyes told her what she wanted to know. He was exhilarated. He belonged to her. 'Yes,' she laughed. 'It did, didn't it?'

'It did. It felt so good to get revenge on those traitors.'

'Come now, we must make haste to Carnelia. We'll fortify its walls. We'll make it impenetrable to our foes. Now that we know there are traitors at every turn, people we once thought we could rely on, we will be on our guard. We only have each other now, brother. We'll protect the city, and ourselves with all our might. Fear will keep the people loyal. Our Azurian army will be feared across the land, with the help of our firefly allies, we will hold the city, and the kingdom for years to come.'

The boy lapped up every word she spoke.

'I want you to name the new city, Alexander. What would you like to call it?'

The boy's eyes widened, and she fancied that she saw actual flashes of joy. She watched him process what she had just told him, as the gears and cogs of his brain turning as he thought of a new name for the city of Carnelia. Eventually, his childish grin returned. He looked at her, and his blue eyes had never looked so deep, so sharp.

'I want to call it, The City of the Fireflies,' he announced.

Endellion laughed. 'So be it, brother. Let us make haste to The City of the Fireflies!'

~~~~

Of course, Alexander saw Cassandra laugh.

His face fell for a moment as there was something in her laughter he didn't like. *It looks like someone else laughing,* he thought. He shook his head, hoping to dismiss the small part of him that was still horrified at what they had just done.

'So be it, brother,' his sister shouted as her firefly rose from the ground with a thrum of its powerful wings. 'Let us make haste to The City of the Fireflies!'

He watched as her beast flew off, stopping only once to turn to see where he was.

With a sickening feeling in the pit of his stomach, he commanded his beast to rise and follow, who he thought was his sister, towards their new city.

12.

THAT NIGHT THEY slept in a grassy glade with enough shelter to protect them from the winds and the rain of the cold weather front that had moved in. Alexander had fallen asleep almost straight away. Endellion watched as his chest rose and fell with the deep snores of a child who had been called to be an adult too soon. He'd told her that he felt safe in the knowledge that their firefly army was protecting them.

Long after the boy had fallen into the grip of sleep, she had lain awake. Rest for her was elusive. She felt that everything she had wanted for so long, everything she had ever dreamed of, was so tantalisingly close.

She forced herself to relax and closed her eyes. The elusive sleep proved to be closer than she thought.

As it came for her, her dreams heralded back to her youth.

To her last days in Carnelia.

13.

ENDELLION WAS FIFTEEN and living a life of luxury and privilege within the Carnelian palace as special guest to King Leopold and Queen Rabia. She had lived here all her life and had never known any different. She enjoyed the way the courtesans and staff spoke to her, offering her reverence and bowing and curtsying whenever they saw her. She, however, had never let her privileged position get the better of her. She was as polite and good mannered as she was pretty, and there was always talk around the palace about how close the little Lady Endellion and Prince Thaddius had become.

She always did her best to keep out of the way of King Leopold. There was a coldness about him, mostly towards her. It was as if he didn't want her around, like he feared her for some reason. Sometimes she would find him looking at her. His lip would be curled, and his air would be of someone who looked like they'd bitten into sour fruit.

She didn't mind this as she didn't like him much either.

The queen, however, she was different. Some nights she would call Endellion to her chambers, and they would spend the evening knitting or doing needlework, but mostly they talked. Queen Rabia loved to tell Endellion stories about her and her mother's time together.

They had apparently spent lots of quality time, and she knew a lot about her. She told her that her mother was a noblewoman from a village far away, from a city over the mountains. That she had made the perilous journey with the brave and noble intentions of forging alliances between her people and the kingdoms of Carnelia and Azuria. She had been an envoy of peace and trade.

She told her that her mother had been involved in an altercation, an incident, and that was how she had found herself to be in the hospital, in the bed next to hers.

Her mother's name had been Camarilla.

This had been the most thrilling part of the story. It felt like a jigsaw piece fitting into a picture. It was by no means complete, but just that little bit closer.

She had been travelling home one night from an important meeting regarding the unification of the three kingdoms when she witnessed a woman being beaten in the doorway of a tavern. She had stepped in, thinking the attacker would not harm a noble lady, and a pregnant one at that. But she had been wrong. The men beating the woman turned on her and pushed her. She fell into a small ravine.

When she was pushed, it caused complications within her womb. She was told it would best for the child if she took complete bed rest. She agreed to be hospitalised for the rest of her term. That was how she was introduced to Queen Rabia, and how they became fast friends.

'Did they ever catch the men who pushed her?' Endellion asked every time this topic was brought up.

'Yes, my dear,' the queen continued the lie with a kindly smile. 'Brave King Leopold hunted them down and put them to death. Your mother was truly vindicated.'

This answer always made Endellion smile, but it also made her a little sad for not liking him after his bravery.

The queen then continued, telling her of the complications Camarilla had experienced during her birth and the fact that these had been too much for her body to endure, and she was informed that she would not survive. 'But, before she passed, she asked the biggest favour of the king. She asked him if we would look after her child when she was gone ... and, of course, we did.'

'What about my daddy?' Endellion would sometimes ask. 'Why didn't my daddy come for me?'

The queen would always stall at this question before answering with another lie. She would tell a story about her brave daddy who embarked on the journey across the mountains but was attacked by a wild beast enroute and killed.

She had been taken in by the king and queen and raised as if she were one of their own. The title of Lady Endellion had been bestowed upon her, and she had been given a rightful place in the court of Carnelia.

There, she was a constant companion to the young Prince Thaddius, and for their first fifteen years, they had been all but inseparable.

~~~~

The pair were playing in the archive rooms beneath the castle. This they did most days. Mostly because it was forbidden, as the rooms were dark, dirty, and dangerous. The smell of musk and decay would have been overpowering to anyone else but an excited pair of teenagers. The rooms had an air of dungeons, that no one had stepped foot within for hundreds, if not thousands of years; in truth, there had only been one person who had ventured inside in all that time. That had been Endellion herself, all those years ago, guided by the purple skinned spirit. She had been down to these rooms many times since that first adventure when the king had scolded her so badly.

Today, they were playing their favourite game, hide and go seek. It was a guilty pleasure for them as they knew they were too old to be playing childish games, but they were in no rush to shrug off their childhood so soon.

It was Thaddius's turn to hide and Endellion searched. It annoyed her that Thaddius was notoriously good at this game. She had been searching for him for over an hour, roaming the corridors beneath the castle, not the least bit scared. Her purple skinned guardian, as she had come to think of her, had led her along these tunnels many times, on long nights when sleep had been difficult to come by.

The tunnels were labyrinthian, but she had grown to understand the landscape. All the landmarks she could use to negotiate her way, aided her. She loved it down here. Sometimes during these games, she allowed Thaddius to believe it was his skill at hiding that prolonged them, but really it was her enjoyment at the exploration. There was always another door to open, another room to explore, another adventure to be had.

On this occasion, Endellion found herself in a wing that she had never been in before. Nothing about the backdrop was familiar to her. The walls were darker than the other wings, and the smell was akin to how the garden smelt late at night when sometimes she would go walking alone.

There were a few trinkets scattered about on shelves that stretched along the dark walls. Reaching out in the dim light, she found a series of old lamps. The first was dusty, but she gave it a shake anyway. There was no slush of oil from within, just a dry, scratchy sound. She tried another, and then another. Finally, she found what she was looking for, a lamp with something wet inside. She opened it and sniffed. The stink was pungent, but there was an underlying tang of oil. There was flint on the shelf also. After a few unsuccessful attempts, she finally got the oil to burn.

As the flickering light from the lamp illuminated the room, she scanned the strange setting. The light didn't penetrate much; rather than helping, it created more shadows, and more questions. Nervously, she moved on down the wing.

'Thaddius. Are you here? If you are, can you please come out? Come on now, I yield to your superior hiding skills,' she shouted, half sarcastically, half hoping he would jump out and they could finish the game. She wouldn't admit it, but this wing spooked her, unlike the rest of the rooms she'd explored. *Maybe it's just because my purple friend has never brought me down here before,* she thought.

Holding the lamp higher, she noticed a door maybe thirty yards further down the hallway. It was ever so slightly ajar.

It looked cleaner than everything else in the corridor.

With trepidation, she stepped towards the thin crack in the door and shone the lamp into the room beyond. A bright glare flashed back at her, taking her by surprise, and she had to step away, shielding her eyes. She slipped on a loose bit of flooring and almost dropped the lamp.

Her eyes eventually got used to the glare, and she removed her hand, allowing herself to gaze on it. It looked to her like every colour of the rainbow had converged and wrapped her in a strangely comforting glow.

When she could open her eyes fully, she couldn't understand what had caused the glare. She peered back inside to investigate the phenomenon. What she saw took her breath away. The multi-coloured effect had been caused from her light reflecting into a room that was filled almost floor to ceiling with every gem she could imagine. There were jewels of every colour and every size! Bright glittering diamonds, some of them the size of her fist. Rubies, sapphires, emeralds, jades. There were rings, necklaces, crowns, tiaras, sceptres. There was more wealth than Endellion could have ever even imagined.

As she stepped inside, a strange buzz bathed her skin. She felt it in her bones, in her stomach, even in her teeth at the back of her mouth. It made the hairs on her arms stand up. It was the strangest feeling she had ever felt. As she stepped deeper into the room, the feeling intensified. Then, almost as suddenly as it started, it stopped.

It felt as if the room had dulled. The shine from the jewels and treasures had reduced, significantly. Young Endellion found herself staring at an old, dusty grey wooden box. It was the one dull thing in the room, but there was something special about it, something she couldn't put her finger on. She felt as though the box was calling to her. The sweet siren song making her long to open it, to immerse herself in its delights.

She didn't know if this was a good feeling, or if it was evil, but a lust enveloped her, driving her towards the old, shabby box.

She had to open it, there was simply no other choice.

So, she did.

Putting the lamp down, she fumbled with the latch of the box. It was stiff and rusted with age, but eventually, it opened enough for her to look inside. It was too dark to see anything, so she shone the lamp. Truthfully, she was disappointed with what she saw. Nestled within the dark box was a small, dull grey ball.

Everything about it was unremarkable, but the urge to pick it up, to hold it in her hands, was unsurmountable. She held her breath while reaching in and picking it up.

The exact moment her fingers wrapped around it, a cold shiver ran up her arm, causing her skin to breakout in goosebumps; these bumps travelled all over her body. As she gripped it, attempting to pick it up, the strangest thing happened, and she didn't know if she should drop it and run or hold it tighter.

The ball began to glow.

The glow was a deep red.

As it throbbed, for reasons she couldn't understand, she closed her eyes. Instantly, she was in another place. It was an old, dark room. The chamber was vast and gloomy and smelt of age and decay. The only furniture was a large altar. On top of this lay something she had no desire to investigate further.

A noise from behind her startled her, and she turned to see where it had come from. An old man with long white hair that blended into his long white beard was looking at her.

He was smiling.

Stepping back from the vision, she lost her grip on the orb, and it fell. The moment it left her hands, the glow dulled, and the ball became an uninteresting grey again.

The second surprise, the one that caused her to scream a little and step back, was that Thaddius was standing before her, his form silhouetted by the light of the lamp. As she stepped back, she knocked the lamp over. It tipped and spilled its oil over the table and floor. Then the oil caught fire. The illumination instantly dimmed in tandem with the glow from the fire. They both panicked and began to smother it using all they had to hand—their clothes. They didn't trust using any of the old rags that were lying around in-between the treasure.

'Thaddius,' she scolded, as the oil began to burn itself out into a harmless blue light. 'You scared me. Look what you've done now. I can hardly see anything.'

What she *could* see was his intense smile, made even more dangerous and thrilling by the shadow covering his face.

'Don't worry,' he chided. 'I've got a spare lamp just over here.' He took her hand and guided her towards the other side of the room. As their fingers intertwined, she felt the second strange sensation of the evening. This was more delightful than the first.

It was not to be the last.

A chill ran through her body. It was not an unpleasant feeling, but strange. It culminated in the pit of her belly.

'What's the matter, Endellion? Are you coming or what?' Thaddius asked as he pulled her towards him.

'Yes, I—' She never got to finish her sentence, as her best friend pulled her towards the lamp, and him. Her foot slipped on a golden plate on the floor. As she fell, he caught her in his arms. She had never been in his arms before. They had fought as children and tussled on the floor, but she had never been held by him. *He's stronger than he looks,* she thought.

Before she knew it, before any other thoughts could run through her head, his lips were on hers. With no thought of protest or chastity, she returned the embrace.

It was light at first, but it intensified the longer it continued. When she realised what they were doing, she was so shocked by her brazenness that she tightened up.

'I'm … I'm sorry, Endellion…' he stuttered, pulling away from her. 'I just … thought …'

The delightful tingle of her very first kiss still lingered on her lips, As he pulled away, her eyes were still closed.

All thoughts of the old man she had seen while holding the grey ball were gone.

She opened her eyes. The shiver that had begun in her belly reverberated through her body, lighting up sensations in places she had never realised could even have feelings. 'That's the problem,' she whispered, breathlessly. 'You think too much.' She then leaned back into him, stretching on her tiptoes, and kissed him back.

Their embrace was filled with all the long passion of youth and first love. Thaddius was clumsy and fumbling, and Endellion too self-aware, but they were enjoying themselves, immensely.

When the kiss was over, his fingers gently traced the contours of her face, sending little thrills across her skin.

'Do you think we should go back now?' he whispered. She thought she could sense more than a hint of disappointment and anticipation in his voice.

'I think we should,' she replied, sensing the frustration in her *own* voice. A smile broke on her lips as her brown eyes looked up at him.

'But,' she whispered shyly. 'Maybe we could play this same game, tomorrow. What do you think?'

'I think we could,' he chuckled. 'And the day after, and the day after that too.'

Both of their faces beamed as he grabbed the lamp and offered his arm to help her through the room. They made their way back along the corridor holding hands.

As she left the room, she offered one last glance towards the drab, ordinary grey ball lying on the floor next to the jewelled table.

Part 4

01.

CASSANDRA WAS IN the chambers she had been allocated on the successful occupation of Outpost Three. She was alone, practising with her Glimmer. The ball was in her hand, creating a warm blue around the room. Her eyes were closed, and her mouth cut a thin white slash across her face. She was determined to master control over these damned butterflies, even if she died trying. So far, she had managed only a modicum of success. Two small blue creatures had fluttered around her head before landing on a shelf, as she had instructed them to do. However, from there, it had all gone wrong. The totems had then broken free of her control, fluttering about haphazardly before disappearing almost as quickly as they appeared. Her control had lasted for a little over two minutes.

Her Glimm guide was in her head. This she had mastered. If she needed any of them while she was stuck in the real world, she could summon their voices just by holding the Glimmer and thinking about them.

'Patience ...' the voice spoke in good humour. '...and dedication, child. Patience and dedication.'

This had become the mantra of her guide over the few days.

'Do you think the Great Lord Glimm became the master of all he surveyed overnight? No, child, he had patience, dedication, and faith!'

'I know all this,' she replied with an exhaustive breath. 'I just think if I could get a grip on what is possible with this thing, then it would benefit our cause.' Her face flushed in annoyance. She put all her concentrated effort back onto the orb, and a small, pathetic looking butterfly appeared. It fluttered around the room, bumping into the walls. Her tongue lolled out of the side of her mouth.

'Patience, dedication, faith, and humility. They are all you need to master the Glimm. Patience, dedication, faith, humility, and tenacity.'

Cass was grinning as she opened her eyes. 'You're just making all of this up, aren't you? You add a new word each time.'

Her guide continued, although she could hear the humour in his voice, 'Patience, dedication, humility, tenacity, and obedience ...'

Cass laughed, and as she did, something strange, and equally fantastic, happened.

As the chuckle left her mouth, a flurry of the most beautiful blue butterflies appeared as if on her breath. Once free, they fluttered around her head, each acting as if they were in thrall to her.

'Did I do that?' she giggled.

'Well, if you have to ask that question, then maybe you are not even a little bit ready for the power you already wield.'

'Oh no, I *am* ready,' she gushed. 'I just wasn't expecting it, that's all.'

'If you weren't expecting it, then why did you do it? It will obey your commands at any specific time. You made it happen, Cassandra. You have to be careful what you want, because now you hold the power to receive it.'

'With great power comes great responsibility,' they both recited at the same time, laughing.

A number of the larger butterflies rested on her outstretched hand, and her face changed. Her eyes clouded, and a darkness overshadowed the playful delight they held moments earlier. 'Can you tell me of Endellion?' she asked, not really believing the question had come from her. She swallowed hard, then continued. 'Can you tell me what she wants? Why she is how she is?' As she moved her hand down to caress the glowing ball in her lap, the butterflies dissolved into the air. She grasped the Glimmer in both hands, closed her eyes, and was instantly back in the large, musty altar room of The Glimm.

'You know I cannot discuss the other custodian of the Gimmer. We are as enthralled to her as we are to you.'

Cassandra frowned and sat on the nave of the altar. 'Do you guide her as you do me?'

The old man offered her a fatherly frown before allowing himself to sigh a deep, sorrowful breath. He nodded slowly. 'We do,' he said, closing his eyes as if to ward off a vision he no longer wanted to see. 'It was a very long time ago, in your time. We gave her guidance, as I do you now. All I can tell you is that she was a natural with the orb. It was almost as if she were born to wield it. She took to the training instantly, and the training took to her.' He stopped talking for a moment, taking the time to look at Cassandra. The intense scrutiny made her feel more than a little awkward. 'When I think about the both of you,' he continued. 'You are very similar. It is almost as if the battle between you and her was meant to be. Although, if it was written, then we would surely know the outcome. Alas, we do not.'

'Will I become as proficient as her with my Glimmer? I ask only because The Ferals and The Rebels are outnumbered in our fight against her. We are only a small force, winning small victories here and there. Every man lost is a blow to our cause.'

The Glimm looked at her and smiled; it was a kindly smile. 'You will only become as proficient as her with patience, dedication, humility, tenacity, obedience, and understanding ...'

Cass laughed aloud at the old man's attempt at levity to diffuse the gloomy conversation. 'You just added another one ...'

A loud banging noise disturbed her concentration. She recognised it as a knocking on her door.

'Cass, Cassandra, are you in there?' The shout, from somewhere in space around her, entered her ears. It was a strange feeling, hearing something that was happening in a different environment, in a different reality, it gave her a sense of disorientation. She opened her eyes and saw

173

she was surrounded by all the trimmings and entrapments of the chambers she had been assigned. She sighed, more in relief than anything else.

'Are you in there, Cassandra?' the voice shouted again. The muffled nature of it told her that it was coming from the other side of the door. 'We need to talk.'

It was Bernard, and he sounded worried.

She ran to the door, unlocked it, and threw it open. *What's wrong with me?* she thought. *Every time I see him these days, my heart beats that little bit faster...* She didn't fool herself into thinking she wasn't already in love with him, but the timing of it just wasn't right.

When is it right? she thought with a wry smirk.

Bernard fell through the door; he was flushed and breathless. 'Cass, we need to talk. I've just had word from the Rebels. They've sent a messenger with talk of their camp being attacked and decimated by fireflies. There's been multiple casualties.'

Cassandra frowned, the wrinkles on her forehead ran deep. 'Do we know how many? Do we know who's dead?'

'No. All we know is that the camp is gone. It sounds like the fireflies killed the prisoners too.'

'Can we send any word to the survivors? To get them to the safety of this castle?' she asked hopefully.

Bernard shook his head. 'Unfortunately not, they've gone underground. There is a network of tunnels, hundreds of years old. Our messengers will never locate Ambric if he's gone dark. He's too good.'

'In that case, I think we need to fortify our location here. Make it a base of operations. It looks like this outpost can be defended, from a normal attack at least. We'll have to sniff out any secret passages in and out that could be exploited and used against us,' she replied.

'Agreed. I'm going to send a small party to attempt to locate the Rebels, even though I think it will be a folly; but if they need help, then we should be in a position to offer it, if and when they reach out for us.'

'That's a good idea. Do you have any idea where the tunnels might lead?'

Bernard shook his head. 'Not a clue. Ambric will though. He has extensive knowledge of the area. But as I said, if he's decided to go dark, then it'll be interesting to see where they do emerge.'

'Bernard, there's something I want to show you. It's … erm,' Cass stuttered, changing her mind halfway through her telling Bernard about her secret.

He looked at her, his face a mask of confusion. 'What is it, Cass?' he asked, turning away from her, about to leave her chambers.

'Oh, nothing.' she said, waving him away. 'Nothing that can't wait, that is.' She smiled. He returned in kind before leaving the room.

She harrumphed as she sat down on her bed. She had so wanted to tell Bernard about her butterflies, but she was not sure how he would take the news that she was gaining the same powers as their enemy. No, her reveal would have to wait. 'Maybe I should just tell him I'm falling in love with him too,' she laughed to herself and blushed.

'Falling in love with who?' came a voice from behind the door.

175

Cassandra's eyes went wide as she turned to face whoever had walked in her chambers unannounced. She was mortified to see that it was Bernard. He was wearing a large, almost conceited grin on his face. 'Who's falling in love with who, Cass? Come now, I need to know. A leader needs to know if there's any romances blossoming within his camp,' he teased.

Her face burned; she imagined it had turned purple as he asked the searching questions. She tutted as she blustered past him, towards the door, muttering. 'Bernard, you can be such a bastard sometimes, you know.'

As the door slammed, it was Bernard's turn to harrumph as he sat down heavily on her bed.

2.

WITH CARNELIA IN sight, Endellion decided to dismiss the fireflies and walk the last mile into her kingdom. She wanted to create the illusion of tiredness and raggedness, as if they had only just escaped the ambush of Outpost Three.

'But, Cass, I'm tired enough as it is. Why can't we enter into our own Kingdom in the luxury we are accustomed to?'

Listen to him, she thought. '*Our kingdom.*' *I'm doing such a good job of turning you, my young boy, into my biggest ally.* She laughed as the thoughts ran through her head, watching the boy struggle to dismount his firefly.

It was obvious there was something troubling him. His head was bowed, and it was clear he didn't want to look her in the eye.

'Cass, can I ask you something?'

'Of course you can, brother. You can always ask me anything,' she replied, offering the youth a friendly smile.

'Why did we attack and kill our own men?' he asked. 'They were prisoners.'

The question shocked Endellion, but it made her happy he was asking these questions. It gave her the opportunity to fill his young head with her own propaganda. 'Alexander, it's a well-known fact that when prisoners are taken, sometimes their captors turn their heads with small mercies and kindnesses. It was my belief that was happening in the camp. Those men could never again be trusted. We would have been constantly watching our backs around them,' she lied, hiding the smile on her face. 'Tell me, though, brother, how did it feel? How did it feel to have the power of life and death over those men at your hands? Real lives hanging on your decisions. Did it make you feel … godlike?'

The boy fell silent as they walked towards their destination. For the last mile, they walked side by side in silence.

As the portcullis on the walls of Carnelia loomed, Alexander reached out his hand and grabbed his sister's arm, stopping her in her stride.

They looked into each other's faces.

'Yes, sister. I did enjoy the feeling.' He bowed his head as if making a solemn confession. 'It did make me feel godlike.'

Endellion's Cassandra face creased as if she was about to cry. She wiped the crocodile tears from her face and held her arms out to the young boy who thought he was her brother. 'That is good, Alexander. It's good because there's going to be a lot more of that to come. There'll be tough decisions, there'll be bloodshed, and there may well even be suffering. But remember, brother, you *are* godlike. You have an elevated

178

position in life, you have great power. There'll be many people who will look to take this power away from you. Never, ever allow them to. Many people will lie and cheat and steal to take our positions. These people must be dealt with the same justice that we dealt in that camp. Are you ready for that level of responsibility, Alexander? Do you think you can handle it?'

He smiled as he relaxed into Endellion's embrace. Even though the smile was genuine, there was no twelve-year-old humour in it.

'Yes, Cass. Good things come to those who are willing to wait for it!'

Endellion's face contorted at the odd phrase. Without answering, she shook her head, and they continued their journey.

3.

'OPEN THIS DOOR! Open it up in the name of your queen, Cassandra,' Alexander shouted as he banged on the metal of the portcullis of Carnelia with the hilt of his sword. 'Look down from your towers and see for yourselves. It is us, Queen Cassandra and her brother, Alexander.'

A few confused faces popped, almost comically, over the wall to gaze below. When they saw the pair, they looked at each other, then looked back down again. Then, the heads disappeared back into their towers.

Endellion and Alexander could hear muted shouts and callings from behind the walls. A dispute was running backwards and forwards between men regarding whether it could be them, or not. After almost ten minutes of shouted debate, noises began to filter through from beyond the large wooden door. The sounds of chains being pulled, and the squeal of bolts being retracted.

Finally, the metal gate was raised, revealing the city beyond. Just inside the boundaries stood ten men dressed in the garb of Azurian soldiers. One of them stepped forward and introduced himself.

'My name is Marcus. I'm Captain of the Wall.' He looked at the two dishevelled travellers before him, his eyes flickering between both dirty, tired faces. 'Erm, would you please identify yourselves?' he asked nervously.

Alexander stood forward from his sister and snarled into the soldier's face. 'Marcus,' he growled, sounding much older than his twelve years. 'You would think that rising to the lofty heights of Captain of the Wall, you would be able to recognise the face of your queen! The same queen you pledged allegiance to when you took up arms in the name of Azuria. Gaze upon her now, and her brother Alexander. Recognise us and allow us into our realm.'

The captain's eyes continued to flick between them. His face was pained and more than a little embarrassed. 'Oh, yes, of course, my lord. Please accept my apologies and enter with all graces into your occupied kingdom of Carnelia. I just needed to be sure, as there have been tales regarding a witch in the garb of the queen.'

Alexander's eyes narrowed as he looked at the captain. 'Does my sister, your beloved ruler, look like a witch to you?' He held the man's eye for too long; the soldier was the first to look away.

'Well,' the older man said, shrugging as he regarded the dirty face of his queen. 'She doesn't look like she does on the portraits,' he replied with an embarrassed smile.

181

Alexander rolled his eyes. 'Captain, you will find this out very soon anyway, but you might as well know now. The city is no longer be referred to as Carnelia. From now on it is to be known as The City of the Fireflies.'

'Eh, yes, my lord,' the captain stuttered as he bowed low. 'Please enter your realm of The, erm, City of the Fireflies.'

Alexander and Endellion walked proudly into the courtyard. There were many soldiers on hand to witness the entrance of their queen.

'Captain of the Guard?' Endellion inquired once she was safely inside and the portcullis had been lowered.

The captain scurried up alongside both the newcomers. 'Yes, ma'am?'

'I require a room. I require my chambers to be ready for me presently. I am extremely tired, and I desire privacy to rest, and I mean total privacy. No guards, no visitors.'

'Of course, ma'am. We've had your chambers ready for a while, as we were expecting you yesterday. I'll call your chambermaids and ladies; they will attend you and make you comfortable.' He gestured towards one of his men and pointed him away in the direction of the main castle. The man ran off fast. Within a few moments, he returned with four women, all, including the soldier, were out of breath and looked scared half to death.

'Ma'am.' The oldest of the women curtsied. 'I am Magda. I'm to be your head maid during your stay here. If you would be so kind to follow me, I'll show you to your prepared chambers.'

Endellion gestured to the ladies, and they all walked off towards the castle. She turned towards Alexander as she left, offering him a nod and a conspiratorial wink. He nodded back curtly.

When they were gone, Alexander turned his attentions back to the captain. 'I require the guard on the city walls to be tripled. I want this city to become a fortress.'

'Yes, sir, not a problem. There is just one thing. You were expected yesterday, and we've had no word from Outpost Three. We feared the worst. We were drawing up a host to ride and see if there had been trouble between there and here.'

'Well, sir, let me tell you, there was. When we reached Outpost Three, they were waiting for us. Somehow, these Ferals, or Rebels, or whatever they're calling themselves, had taken the castle. The queen and I smelled a rat prior to our approach. It was obvious that someone within the ranks had leaked information, so we held back. It was a good thing we did too. When the trap was sprung, we managed to slip away.'

Many of the soldiers had gathered around the boy to hear the tale and were drinking in every word of the lie. As there had been poor communications between the camps for the last few days, nobody was any the wiser.

'I fought off a number of them myself,' he continued to brag. 'Before we were forced to retreat, mainly due to the number of Rebels attacking. We watched as our escorts were either slaughtered or taken prisoner. We'll need the guard of the watch tripled, as it is mine and your queen's belief that these men may have somehow been hypnotised or brainwashed into changing sides. Again, this is something we have personally witnessed. What remains of our escort may still ride to our doors attempting to gain entry. If they do, do not allow them in. They are not to be taken prisoner to spread their filthy lies, do you hear me? I'll have no insurrection in my City of Fireflies.'

The captain stood alert. his body language conveying that he had been buoyed by the tale, the lies, spewing from the young boy's mouth. 'Yes, sir,' he snapped. 'Your order has been given. I'll send for men to be sent from Azuria. They will each be given a special password so we'll know it is them. Consider it done, my lord.'

'Excellent,' Alexander replied with a smirk. 'But we'll not need as many men as you think.'

The captain's face fell at this news. 'My Lord, we're almost stretched to capacity as it is. We have insurgence here, within our walls. I know it's to be expected when occupying a former stronghold of your enemy, but I'm controlling double, sometimes triple shifts as it is. We're running low on supplies, fresh water, emergency services. I *will* require more men and resources if we are to cover the extra shifts you request.'

Alexander shook his head; there was a cock-sure grin on his face as he looked at the worried soldier before him. 'No, Captain, as I say, you'll not need as many as you think.' He stood tall in the middle of the group. Everyone watched as the boy grew in stature before them. He put two of his fingers within his mouth and whistled.

The soldiers looked at each other, confusion filled their faces. The captain's own was a mask of embarrassment as he watched the twelve-year-old boy speak as if he was a man and a soldier.

Then he heard it.

They all heard it.

It began as a small humming sound, way off in the distance. Then it grew. There was a deep resonance that the captain felt within his stomach and in his boots. He regarded the rest of his men. Each was looking up to the sky. There was an air of confusion and fear.

As the sound continued to grow, the beating could be felt in the breeze, like the air itself was alive and pulsing, throbbing like a great drum. From over the walls they came. Their small but powerful wings buzzing in unison.

The soldiers, all of them, watched dumbfounded as a legion of fireflies rose over them like a dark cloud, alive and promising the worst storm ever.

They ascended high with ease. The sight of the beasts terrified the men. Some ran, others held their ground with drawn weapons, but all of them were awed.

The first wave of the beasts flew into the courtyard, soon followed by another wave, then another, and another. Soon there were hundreds of them hovering over the castle grounds. The soldiers stood ready for an anticipated attack.

An attack that didn't happen.

The men who had broken rank at the sight of the monsters stopped. A few of them slinking back into their positions.

'Gentlemen,' Alexander shouted over the thrum of the beating wings. 'Please be the first to meet our latest recruits, and our greatest allies. They are the inspiration behind the name of our new, great city. Behold, the Firefly army!'

The boy was grinning from ear to ear.

'W-w-what are they?' The Captain of the Wall stuttered.

'They are our friends, under the command of me, and your queen of course. They are loyal to the death, and they are fierce. Please treat them with the same respect you offer me and my sister. They are the new guardians of our city.'

4.

ENDELLION LOCKED HERSELF into her new chambers and dismissed the staff. She was feeling tense as she had been in the guise of Cassandra for several days, and her bones were weary. So, with a shiver of delight that was half relief, she reverted to her own image.

She sat in the centre of the room and closed her eyes, gripping her Glimmer firmly in her grasping fingers.

The ball was glowing a deep red.

In her head, she was in the altar room of the Glimm, and again, she was arguing with her guide.

'You *will* show me the way. I demand you to,' she screamed, her voice echoing off the walls of the bare room.

The guide was impassive of her tantrum, his face stoic as he regarded her. 'I cannot show you the physical way. That is something beyond our control. I can guide you on the use of our powers, but I'm afraid I cannot lead.'

Endellion, thinking there was a hint of sarcasm in the man's expressionless face, flew into a rage. 'Why do you defy me at every turn?' she spat, flexing her hands and fingers into tight fists, her long fingernails digging into the flesh of her palms. 'Why do wish to break my spirit?'

The guide did not move as she raged at him, raising her hands like weapons, ready to scratch and tear his face. All he did was watch as she passed through him as if he were a cloud.

Her rage subsided almost as quickly as it had risen.

From the corner of her eye, she could see someone else in the background. She tried hard to focus on who it could be, but she couldn't make it out. What she did understand, though, was the Glimm guide standing before this mysterious person was clearly talking to … *another girl,* she hissed in her head.

'What is going on over there?' she demanded.

The Glimm didn't even turn his head, he just continued to stare at her with his impassive gaze.

'I demand you tell me what is going on back there. Is it an echo of my past dealings?' Her voice wavered in the middle of the question.

'That is something that does not concern you. I'm here to serve, but there are some things I cannot relay,' he replied. His voice was plumy, and she thought she could sense a smirk. This told her he was enjoying frustrating her.

The faint sound of laughter filtered across the room, and she turned to see whoever it was talking with the guide, dancing around as if there was something fluttering around her head. Seeing whoever it was enjoying themselves turned her, and she flew into another rage. 'Tell me who that is and what she is doing. Tell me the way to your altar. I have much unfinished work. Tell me all of this now,' she roared.

Her Glimm guide simply stood and looked at her. 'With regret, I cannot ...'

Endellion seethed. 'When I find your altar,' she hissed between gritted, grinding teeth. 'I'll take both Glimmers and destroy it. I'll banish you and all your spirits to Koll'Su. I'll tear down the very existence of the Glimm. Before I kill you all, I will absorb your powers. I will challenge and defeat the Great Lord Glimm himself.'

When her rant was over, she took a moment to control herself. She leaned into her spirit guide and whispered, making the words sound as sinister as she could. 'I will become *the* most powerful entity in this world, and in the next.'

The guide stood motionless, watching her rant.

She opened her eyes and was back in her chambers. She had brought the anger, frustration, and fatigue back with her, and was suddenly exhausted. With her Glimmer securely tucked in the folds of her outfit, she made sure her door was locked before climbing into her bed. Sleep was needed, desperately, and remaining in her original Endellion form, she slipped between the covers and closed her eyes.

D E McCluskey

5.

SHE SLIPPED FROM the warmth of her winter covers and ran to the door of her room. She grabbed the thickest robe from the rack and quickly wrapped herself in it. Looking out of the frosted window, she had to wipe at the condensation that had built up on the inside. Once it was gone, she put her head to the cold glass and peered outside. The snow was thick, and the wind looked to be whipping up quite a storm.

She peered her head out of the door to her chambers and looked down both sides of the corridor. Because of the early hour, the castle was mostly in darkness, but she could hear the faint sounds of guards laughing in the crude manner men do in the early hours of the morning. She knew she would have no problems sneaking past them, after all, no one would be actively looking for a seventeen-year-old girl in a housecoat, tiptoeing through the castle.

Endellion entered the wing she thought of as *The Purple Wing,* after the spectral figure who had shown it to her all those years ago. It was pitch black, and the smell, if she hadn't had gotten used to it over these last few years, would have probably made her turn back. It was earthy and damp, but she'd come to associate it with pleasant activities, and that made it bearable. Wrapping the housecoat around her a little tighter to stave the biting cold, she counted her steps along the corridor before stopping and feeling around the floor for the trapdoor she knew was there. Finding it, she pulled it open with ease, marvelling at how easy it had become to open it due to its regular use.

Silently, she slipped inside.

Finding the lamp that had been strategically placed on the other side, she struck the flint, and it lit at once. She had made provision there would be enough oil in it, and it had been cleaned so she wouldn't have to spend too much time fussing over it. The light illuminated the gloomy corridor, and she waited a few long moments for her eyes to adjust enough for her to see. Once she was good to go, she saw what she wanted right away. It was the door to the jewel room. Even from out here, she could see the lights, every single colour of the rainbow, playing and reflecting on the jewels inside.

Her heart was beating twice as fast as it should, but then it always did when she came to this room in the dead of night. She tried to be as quiet as she could as she crept along the corridor, smiling as she tiptoed. She knew that right now she would be able sing and shout at the top of her voice while dancing in tap-shoes and nobody would hear her, still she crept. Maybe someone in the kitchens would hear a faint wail and a tapping and think it was the ghost of a scullery maid from long past, doomed to repeat her ghostly duties for all eternity. This thought made her grin widen as she quickened her pace towards her destination. Even though she was silent, she imagined every tiny noise made was like elephants crashing through the kitchen, smashing up crockery and crashing all the metal pans.

As she neared the door, she stubbed her toe. The pain in her digit was almost unbearable, and she had to put her hand in her mouth to stifle the scream. *Who put that there?* she cursed inside her head.

She knew exactly who had left the table there: it had been her. She'd placed it there the last time she was down here to view the jewels. It was there to prop the heavy door open. The first few times she'd been here was to marvel at all the beautiful things there were to see, the greens, yellows, blues, and reds, to hold them in her hands and wear the crowns and tiaras.

Nowadays, there was an ulterior motive. One that she didn't want King Leopold, Queen Rabia, or anyone else, for that matter, to know about. It wasn't the first time she had visited the room for this reason, and she knew in her heart it wouldn't be the last; but it was *such* a guilty pleasure that she felt absolutely no shame in it.

With a glance behind to make sure she hadn't been followed and a small, sly smile on her face, she entered the bright room, the most beautiful chamber she had ever seen.

She knew exactly what she wanted, and she walked over to the small, nondescript wooden box lying on a bejewelled table. She opened the lid and gazed upon the nondescript ball inside. Even though it was probably the dullest object in the room, there was something about it, something that called to her …

Closing the lid, she hid the box on the shelf beneath the table and turned her attention to the pretty jewellery all around. She tied up her long blond hair with a ribbon of the finest silk, embossed with small sapphires. Next, she adorned her head with a matching tiara. It had been forged with a pure white gold frame, with the largest jade she had ever seen in the centre. It was much heavier than it looked. She then clipped in the earrings that made a set with a necklace of tight clustered diamonds on a white gold and silver chain. She picked up a jewel-embossed hand mirror from the table and held it before her, posing within the strange multicoloured hues of the room.

'It's perfect.' A voice from behind startled her.

She froze.

A guilty feeling of being caught in the act of doing something she was not supposed to be coursed through her body, and her already racing heart began to beat even faster. A face came into view in the mirror behind her. It was a man's face, obscured just enough in shadow for her not to be able to make it out.

She turned.

As she did, her robe opened at the front and fell to the ground. Underneath, she was as naked as the day she had been born, save for the ancient, and exotic, jewellery that adorned her body. The jewels created delicious shades in the dancing flames of her lamp.

'I'm glad you approve … My Prince,' she replied, her voice taking on a seductive, silky tone.

'Oh, I do,' Thaddius replied as he walked into the light of the lamp. He was smiling as he took her naked body in his arms and kissed her.

6.

CASSANDRA WAS ALONE. She had been practicing with her Glimmer all afternoon, and her butterflies were starting to behave themselves nicely. She had learned how to tap into other guides' powers and was fascinated with the ability of remote seeing, which allowed her to see what was happening in other parts of the castle.

She could see the guards of the watch on their breaks, drinking tea and heating up potatoes for their meals. She could hear them having in-depth conversations regarding what they witnessed in the courtyard a few days ago, about witches who were able to change their appearance, or even the appearance of others, seemingly at will. It was a conversation that worried her. It was filled with paranoia, and she knew only too well that paranoia fuelled fear.

She had a small devious plan devised in which she was going to give some of the men a playful scare with one of her butterflies, but she had second thoughts as, in an atmosphere such as this, it might have begun a chain of events they could do without.

There was nothing she could do with the information she had retrieved since she had decided not to tell anyone about the depth of powers of her Glimmer offered, at least for the time being. Telling someone what the men were thinking would likely get her labelled as much of a witch as Endellion. Until such a time when she needed tell, the paranoia regarding what Endellion could and could not do would only rise. She needed to decide.

Frustrated, she left her chambers to find Bernard.

She had hoped to use the powers of the Glimm to locate Ambric and his men. But, alas, she didn't seem to have the scope for that … not yet anyway. So, she was left with the unsettling knowledge of what their own men were thinking.

Bernard was in the courtyard, running drills with the men, when he saw Cassandra approach. He broke off, instructing Matthew, his second in command to take charge. His friend glanced in the direction Bernard was looking and smirked.

'No worries. Just don't do anything … stupid, eh?' he laughed.

Bernard gave him a friendly punch on the arm. 'I won't,' he grinned walking off.

'Cass, what's wrong? You look like you've got the weight of the world on your shoulders.'

All she could offer him was a worried smile and a shake of her head. 'Sometimes, I think I have. It pains me that so many people have died in my name, albeit my false name. There must be people out there who hate me, who wish me dead.'

'Stop berating yourself,' he replied, putting his arms around her, pulling her in to him for a hug. 'The people *will* know. They'll find out Endellion's evil—'

'Do you have any more intelligence on the whereabouts of The Rebels?' she asked, interrupting him, changing the subject.

It was his turn to shake his head. 'Not yet. We've sent messengers and scouts to cover all of Ambric's known hideouts, but there's nothing to report.'

'I tried to help, but I couldn't see that far ...' she said absently.

Bernard nodded. 'With your Glimmer?' he asked.

She cursed, then snapped back into the conversation. 'I ... erm, I meant that I couldn't think that far ahead. Do you think we should send another party out looking for them? They could be holed up somewhere starving, or worse, they could be dying from their wounds from battle. There must be something we can do.'

Bernard looked at her with his brow creased and his head cocked to one side. 'Cass, the other day you told me that you had something to show me; then you turned coy and ran off. What was that?'

Her face flushed red. *Should I tell him and remove this burden from me? Or do I lie and create a division between us?* she thought. 'I can't tell you right now, not here anyway. If you come to my chambers later tonight, I'll let you into my secret.'

197

Bernard's face lit up, and a goofy smile spread across it. His eyes roamed everywhere as if he didn't know where to allow them to rest.

Cassandra blushed too as she watched his awkwardness. She took in a breath as she realised how her offer could have been construed. She laughed and punched out at his arm. Her fist hit the exact same spot as Matthew's had minutes earlier. 'Not like that, you dirty minded ... boy,' she said, shaking her head and shooing him away.

They were both a little too embarrassed, and a little too excited, to leave.

She eyed him haughtily. 'Later tonight in my chambers, Prince Bernard!' There was an emphasis on the *Prince Bernard* part, as if to remind him who he was and, for that matter, who she was too. 'Come an hour after evening meal, and do not keep me waiting.' There was a large smile on her still reddened face as she walked away from him.

'It's King Bernard,' he said as he watched her go.

~~~~

Later that evening, after their meal, Cassandra was alone again in her chambers, taking the opportunity to practice with her Glimmer. Grim determination was etched into her features as she tried her best to perfect at least one of the powers that the guides had shown her. She could do a little bit of a lot of things, and it was frustrating her.

She longed for the butterflies more than anything else. She didn't know why they were so important to her, but they were. They seemed integral to whatever was going to happen, and she needed to control them correctly.

At present, she had four beautiful specimens in her thrall. Her manifestations were getting bigger and more graceful, and due to her practice, she now had access to them with her eyes open and in this realm, which she thought of as the real world. They were soaring around the room, landing on her hands and head at will. She could get them to work together, to join forces and undergo tasks. She got them to carry a small book from one end of a table to the other. She was exhausted by the time they had completed it, sweating and panting due to her levels of concentration.

Feeling a little overconfident with her technique, she attempted to introduce a fifth butterfly into the mix. When it appeared, it wasn't anywhere near as big as the others, and she found it difficult to control them all. Then, there came a knock on her door, snapping all her concentration away from her task.

Where has all that time gone? she thought as the butterflies began to act erratic. They started flying in random patterns independent of her control and banging into each other. They then began to beat their large wings around the small lamp in the room, but their wings were so large they caused the lamp to fall.

She hurried to the mirror to check on her hair and then straightened her dress. She sighed as she gave her hair one last tousle before responding to the second knock. 'Coming,' she shouted as the butterflies that had been flying haphazardly around the room vanished.

She opened the door and took a quick step backwards, holding her hand to her chest.

Bernard was standing in the corridor holding a large bouquet of flowers. He was wearing the same goofy smile he had worn earlier. 'Erm, these are for you,' he stuttered, pulling on his collar with his free hand, allowing the sweat dripping from his forehead to travel down his neck.

'Where did you get those from?' she asked as she moved away from the door, allowing him inside.

'I … erm, travelled outside the walls. I noticed a field about half a mile from the portcullis on our way here, and I thought they would look … eh, nice, in your room,' he stuttered again, offering her an answer.

Cassandra shook her head. 'Bernard,' she scolded him. 'You shouldn't have put yourself in danger just on my account. You're far too precious to our cause for us to lose you on a folly.' Her reproach was given through a smile. In truth, she thought it was one of the most romantic things anyone could ever done. 'Anyway, now that you're here, you should sit down. I've got something I need to show you.' She guided him towards a two-seated couch by the window and took the flowers from him. She busied herself looking for a vase.

He sat in one corner of the couch, looking like he expected her to sit next to him.

She remained standing. She had found a vase and was pouring water into it.

'Ahem ...' She cleared her throat, trying not to look too bothered that he was sitting in her chambers, looking at her, and smiling *that* smile. 'Bernard, there's something I've been keeping from you for all this time.'

His head cocked very slightly to one side, and she thought she could see concern in his eyes.

'I've kept this from you because, well, because I didn't know how it would be understood by you and The Ferals. I was scared when I was first captured, but then you welcomed me into the group and started to treat me as an equal. So now I have an obligation to show you something that may or may not turn the tides in this war ...'

Bernard sat forward; his dark, intense eyes fixed upon her.

'The very last time I left Azuria, my brother, Alexander, was only a small boy. He was scared. He had just lost his mother; and now his sister, the only tie he had left with his world, was going away too. He handed me a gift, a keepsake, if you like. He told me he'd found it in the caverns beneath the castle and had taken a liking to it. But he wanted me to keep hold of it. To think of him, and home every time I looked at it.'

'Cass, you're not making any sense. You showed us all this Glimmer when we captured who we thought was Endellion,' Bernard interrupted.

She put the vase down on the side-table and gazed out of the window of her chambers. There wasn't much of a view, but it was better than looking at his confused face, *the face I'm falling in love with?* 'I know. But I'm trying to find the best way of telling you what I have.'

Bernard looked a little uncomfortable. 'What you have? This thing hasn't given you a disease, has it?'

She laughed. 'No, silly.' She reached her hand into her hidden pocket and produced the Glimmer. As she brought it forth, it was just a small ball. Dull, blue, and unremarkable. 'It's this.'

Bernard looked at it and shrugged, pouting his lips. 'I thought it was supposed to glow,' he said.

With a smile, she closed her eyes, wrapping her fingers around it, gripping it. The ball responded to her touch by glowing. The blue light poured from between her fingers.

From this close, he noticed it was the same deep blue as her eyes.

'What exactly is it?' he whispered.

She opened her eyes and looked at him. Her expression deadly serious. 'It's called a Glimmer. It's a very old artefact from a different age.'

'I know that, but what does it do?' he asked as he leaned in towards the orb.

'Well, that is what we need to talk about.' She sat down on the seat next to him. Neither of them was nervous of the proximity to each other anymore, there were more pressing matters to discuss. 'There are two Glimmers in existence …' she continued.

'One blue and one red,' Bernard finished for her.

Cassandra nodded. 'They're unique sources of great power. Whoever holds them holds that power. They are free to use them however they see fit; for good or ill. If a person holds both Glimmers, then that person holds ultimate, unrivalled power. There's also an altar and Glimm guides, but we don't need to go into that just yet.'

'Cass, what are you telling me here?'

'I am custodian of one of two Glimmers. This is it, here. I'm still learning how to use it. We both know who holds the other one; the red one.'

'Endellion?' he whispered, not removing his eyes from the glowing ball.

Cassandra nodded. 'She has held the red Glimmer for many years. She has managed to unlock more potential in it than I've been able to gleam from this one. She has used hers to impersonate me, to cause the devastation of your kingdom. I don't know how, but my guide has intimated this.'

Bernard was sat in silence. His face expressionless, but she knew it was his look of shock, or confusion, maybe even both.

Finally, after a long, awkward pause, he spoke. 'You think this little thing could cause all the damage that has been poured upon Carnelia? A little ball?' He was snarling by the time he had finished the question.

'Yes,' Cass replied, dropping her eyes to look at it nestled in her hand.

'And you've had it, literally in your hands, this whole time?'

'Yes,' she replied again.

Bernard stood up and walked over to the window without looking at her. He stopped, gazing out, looking at the same view she was looking at moments earlier.

'You have to understand, I thought it was just a trinket, a nice glowing prize; something to remember my sweet little brother by. Using her Glimmer, Endellion imprisoned me and took my form. This helped me escape. I still don't know how I did it. I'm trying to control it, but it's so difficult. There's so much to learn.' She could hear herself pleading and didn't like it. Add to that, that she could see a rage building up in Bernard as he gripped the sill of the window. Her reveal wasn't going to plan.

'Do you think it has the power to restore what has already been done?'

She took a moment before speaking, surprised to feel tears welling in her eyes. 'I think it has the potential to,' she replied.

Bernard's face softened, and she sighed. He looked at her, he was difficult to read. There looked to be too many emotions passing over, and through him. 'Cass, I'm sorry if I scared you. This is a lot to take in. It is a difficult thing to learn that something with the same power as the witch is sitting here, in the hands of someone I care about.'

'I know,' she replied, trying to wipe tears away without him noticing. 'Why do you think I delayed telling you about it? I need time to master it before I can even think about using it against her.' She smiled, and her face brightened a little. 'Come, sit and I'll give you a small demonstration of what I *can* do.'

He sat on the edge of the couch looking confused, like his head was lost in a whirl. She understood that look; she had worn the same one for the last year or so.

'It's my belief there is a, what I like to call a thrall, to each Glimmer. We've already witnessed the monstrous fireflies Endellion uses for her purposes. Well, it seems I have something like that, too.'

'You have fireflies?' he asked, suddenly animated and excited.

She shook her head. 'Sadly, no. Mine are butterflies.' She almost laughed, more from her nervousness than from humour, at the disappointment on his face.

'Butterflies?' he uttered. There was distaste, and disappointment in his eyes.

She smiled and nodded. 'Butterflies! I've been able to command animals to do my bidding, to a fashion, for a little while now. I don't have the same level of control over these animals as I do over my butterflies.'

Bernard tried unsuccessfully to stifle a laugh. 'What use are butterflies, Cass?' he mocked. She didn't think he meant to, but his words stung her. 'Butterflies are not going to be able to do the same things that we've seen those fireflies do.'

'That's as may be, but watch this ...'

Cassandra closed her eyes and gripped the Glimmer again. As she did, it began to glow, deeper this time. Bernard's eyes widened as he watched a blue butterfly materialise out of nowhere and flutter about his head. Instinctively, he lifted his arm to swat it. He hadn't realised there were four more in the room. They all looked of the same species, but these were larger than the first, the biggest ones he had ever seen. Their wings were the span of each of his arms at least, and they were the same deep blue as Cass's eyes.

'Whoa,' he uttered, standing from the couch. His face resembled that of a child on the opening of brightly wrapped gifts on the Winter Solstice. The awe became amazement as all four butterflies landed on him. He held his arms out, allowing the gentle beasts to perch. He could feel the strength of their legs grip his sleeve and his arm underneath it. His tunic began to pull as the creatures began to tug him. The next thing he knew, he was floating around the room, held only by the four majestic insects. They carried him around before laying him gently back down next to her on the couch.

His mouth was still hanging gape, and Cassandra could see the delight in his wide, glassy eyes. She looked at him and smiled. *I think he realises that could be an asset and not a threat. That* I'm *an asset.*

Bernard was laughing when he threw his arms around her and hugged her tight. He then slapped her on the back in a playful way, the way men do with their friends.

He pulled away from her, still laughing, and suddenly … kissed her.

She blinked and instinctively pulled away.

As did he.

An awkward silence passed between them as they realised one of them had done something they had both wanted to do for a long time.

They stared into each other's eyes for what seemed like an eternity. In real life, it may have only been seconds, but in those seconds, Cassandra realised everything that she needed to know about him. She loved the way he looked back at her. It was as if his soul was standing naked before hers, offering himself to her, complete with all his vulnerabilities.

She liked everything she saw, so, leaning back in, she kissed him.

He kissed her back.

Before either of them realised it, they were falling about on the bed, still kissing and trying their best to rip each other's clothes from their bodies.

Meanwhile, the Glimmer, discarded on the floor, continued to glow a deep blue.

7.

AMBRIC AND HIS Rebels were trapped. He had led them into a labyrinth of tunnels and had quickly gotten them lost. He'd used these tunnels during manoeuvres in his youth in the Carnelian Royal Guard, but it had been many years since he had ventured into them. Back then, he knew them like the back of his hand, every turn, every dead end, every landmark; but like everything in his life, it had changed, and not for the better. Now he was stuck down here, leading a band of fugitive rebels and misfits into Glimm only knew what future.

As he lay awake on a makeshift bed in the small camp they had set up, he reflected on why they were running. Was it possible to fight against something that could reduce a whole kingdom to ruins in less than a day? Would it be worth even trying to build a resistance to a force that had control over a host of monstrous beasts like those fireflies? A force that could imitate a queen and turn a whole kingdom against its neighbours at a whim? 'I don't know anything anymore. Why am I running? Hiding? Is it all for nothing?' he whispered in the dim light of his candle flame.

'Robert? Are you awake?' Gerard, his second in command, whispered to him from the bed on the other side of the room. 'You're mumbling. Is everything OK?'

With sleep so far away from him, Ambric thought it prudent to get himself out of bed. He stretched, ran his fingers through his long hair and beard, and stood up. He made his way out of the small area that he shared with several other soldiers, rubbing the small of his back as he went. He stepped outside the area, and a young boy of maybe seven ran past him with a ball. He and another boy were playing a game where they were trying to get it from each other using only their feet. For several moments, Ambric watched them play. One of them had the ball and the ascendency, then the other, then there was parry and yield and no real winner, as far as he could see. But there was spirit, and it was in abundance. The young boys were both eager to get the ball, both had a respect for the other player, and neither wanted to quit.

The gameplay brought home to him his responsibility to this group. None of them, including himself, had asked for this situation. None of them needed it, but what every single last one of them did not want to do, was give up.

They could have curled up into small human balls and died in the sacking of Carnelia. But no, they had opted to fight, and it was up to him to lead them in that fight. How dare he harbour thoughts of giving up, of retreating, of surrendering to the enemy. These people looked to him in their hour of need. And how funny it was that now he was looking to them, to two young boys playing with a ball, to inspire him in his desperate hour.

He made a decision. His pledge was that as long as there were men left to fight with, and for, then he, Robert Ambric of Carnelia, would be there to guide them in any way he knew how. He would not rest until Carnelia was freed from the tyranny of Endellion.

'Gerard,' he called as he re-entered the sleeping chamber.

'Yes, sir?' came the reply.

He was glad of a man like Gerard at his side. He was always alert, always ready to jump into whatever pit Ambric needed him to.

'Are we ready to give the order to ship out? It's about time we got out of these Glimm-awful tunnels and get ourselves some daylight, and fresh air. What do you say?'

Gerard looked up from the bed he had been relaxing on. A sleepy smile stretched across his face. 'Sir, I think that's the best idea you have had in days.'

'Stop calling me sir.'

8.

'WHERE IS IT?' Endellion shouted, although to anyone listening, of which there was only one person, it sounded more like a scream. She stomped through the corridors and hallways of the castle, her face twisted into a distortion that made her look more like her original form than the beautiful Cassandra she was imitating.

So much had changed since she had left Carnelia. She thought she would be able to remember where the trapdoor to the old corridor leading to the jewel room was. But there had been much refitting in the passing years. Walls had been erected, corridors had been blocked off, and rooms had been knocked through. She felt she could be in a different castle entirely to the one she had memories of growing up in, fond or not.

Alexander was tagging behind her; he had been a constant companion for the last hour or so. 'Why are you following me?' she snapped. 'Do you not have other things to do than bother me like a lost puppy?'

The young boy took the insult in his stride. Endellion had noted a steel in him of late, like he was growing into a man. 'I'm a knight of the realm, sister, and you made me Captain of the Guard. I'm sworn to protect you, and I'll perform my duty until told otherwise,' he replied stoically.

'Well in that case, brother, you are relieved. Now shoo and leave me be,' she replied absently.

The boy bowed low and marched off in the opposite direction. 'I will leave you be, but don't come running to me if you get lost.' The way he marched off was comical to Endellion, and if she were not in such a bad mood, she might have laughed.

Free to continue her search alone, she could feel rage bubbling just below the surface. This was mostly due to the frustration of not remembering where she was. *How long has it been since I was last here?* she thought. She stopped stomping for a moment and thought. *Twenty-five years, maybe more?*

With a frustrated sigh, she sat on the floor in the middle of a particularly derelict corridor. She looked around, making sure that Alexander was really gone and she was indeed alone. Once satisfied, she removed the Glimmer from her secret folds, closed her eyes, and was instantly back in the ancient altar room.

Her guide was stood patiently waiting for her.

'I need to find the passageway to the old chief's meeting room. I know it's here somewhere, but there have been renovations and I can't find it. I need access to it now.'

The Glimm stood and looked at her impassively. 'The room has not moved. You already know where it is. You've been there before. I can see it.'

Endellion glared at the obtrusive man. 'I know I've been there before,' she snapped. 'I need help getting there now. I'm lost in this forsaken castle and in need of your assistance.'

'All you need to do is remember; remember who you were back then and remember who showed you the way in the first instance. Remember!'

Endellion did her best to remember, but all she could recall was that it was a lady, a purple lady. She opened her eyes and was instantly back in the dank, musty corridor. She cast her mind back to the last time she had seen the purple skinned lady. Endellion had been in desperate need of shelter, of somewhere safe to run.

The same could be said now.

She had a desperate need to find the Throne of Glimm. If she was to become all powerful and control both kingdoms, then finding the altar was paramount to her plans.

As she looked deep into the Glimmer, she noticed in her peripheral vision a deep purple glow coming from one of the doors. She stood and made her way to where the glow issued. Her hand was shaking as she reached out for the handle. She grasped it but was disappointed to find it locked. She closed her eyes and visualised the door open. Suddenly, there was a clicking noise, and it swung open. As it did, she watched as the purple glow disappeared around a corner. The light wanted her to follow it, and she acted on that impulse, following the purple wisp through the darkened room. The light was always at least ten yards in front of her, and it kept good pace. Try as she might, she could not keep up with it, or catch it. The glow wound through many different rooms and corridors that she didn't recognise, opening door after door for her.

Suddenly, she was in a corridor she recognised. The bleak and aged décor of the walls told her it was highly likely this corridor had not been used since the last time *she* had been here.

The purple wisp hovered over an area of the floor. She knew exactly what it was showing her. It was the trapdoor she had been seeking, the one that led to another, even danker corridor.

She was eager to enter the trapdoor, but she took a moment to breathe, to take in her surroundings. The location brought memories from her childhood rushing back. Memories that were tinged with elation, excitement, melancholy, and of course, dread.

Putting them to one side, for just the moment, she watched as the purple glow disappeared through the trapdoor. Endellion knew it wanted her to follow, she also knew there was no way she wasn't going to. Everything she had ever wanted, or needed, would be found through that door. *The source of unlimited power,* she thought. She knew the way to the old throne room was mapped out before her, and that map would show her the way to the second Glimmer. She bent, located the rusted old ring, and pulled the trapdoor open. She remembered the times her and Thaddius had played down here. When they were older, they had played different kinds of games. She also remembered the trapdoor had been easier to open back then. *Through constant use,* she grinned.

For the first time in years, it was a sweet smile.

Once the trap was open, she wasted no time entering the purple tinged darkness.

Inside, other than the weak purple glow, it was as black as death. A thought she remembered from her youth. One she had used going into this trapdoor for the first time, a lifetime ago.

As she dropped into the blackness, she smelt the wet, earthy stink that she found both familiar and reassuring. Removing her Glimmer, she willed it to glow; and it did, creating a deep red illumination, not too dissimilar to the purple glow that had led her down here.

She now knew the way.

Continuing down the tunnel as it gently sloped into the cold earth, she felt ground beneath her turn from stone and concrete to clay, chalk, and finally dirt. The further she went, the colder it became, and the stink of damp soil filled her nostrils. She enjoyed the way her breath plumed before her, streaming from her each time she breathed.

After a while, the glow from her Glimmer became brighter as she neared her intended destination. The light illuminated the drawings and pictures on the walls as she spun, enjoying the majestic, old glory of the original throne room of Carnelia.

Endellion's Cassandra form began to shimmy in the red light as she reverted to her natural image. She wanted to re-experience this place, to feel as many emotions run through her as had happened the other times she had entered this revered location.

Mostly awe and terror.

She traced her hands over the walls, enjoying the cold wet feel of the clay as it crumbled and flaked beneath her fingers. She could feel the power of the room, exactly how it had been back then. Power that had passed down from leader to leader, from king to son, or daughter throughout the ages.

Moving on, into another part of the room, there were more drawings on the walls. These representations depicted the building of the castle, the digging of the moat. The one constant in all the pictures was the presence of the Glimmer. In the next set of pictures, she could see the completion of the castle and the Glimmer on show in a position of reverence. It appeared that people, many people, flocked to see it.

Then it looked like it was forgotten. In the final set of pictures, there was less and less documentation as the people moved on from this throne room to the more grandiose one within the modern castle.

She could see no more mention of the Glimmer in any of the remaining pictures.

She explored further; she needed to find what she had come back here for. The directions to the Throne of Glimm.

She remembered the smaller, older drawings she could only see when sat on the old throne. So, she did what she did all those years ago and took her position on the ancient chair in the centre of the room. She remembered the way the uncomfortable chair dug into her skin as she squirmed, attempting to find a little comfort in the chair.

Then she saw what she had come for.

Underneath the other, larger drawings were the directions she craved. The figures that had been painstakingly carved into the wall and the wood, depicting the journey of the old men of the Glimm in loving detail. Following the traveller back to where he had come from.

Endellion got up from the throne and crouched to view these depictions closer. There were other, even smaller carvings beneath these.

They depicted two of the bearded men—one of them had red hair, the other had blue—killing themselves in what looked like a ritual. *They must be the skeletons on the altar*, she thought with a smile. *This is it. It's what I've been looking for. I'll now have the power I've craved since I was expelled. Revenge will be mine.*

As she sat back on the old wooden throne, a wicked smile snaked its way across her lips.

9.

THE DOOR TO the chambers was locked, and the curtains were drawn, even though it was the middle of the day. The chambermaids had been ordered not to clean the room today.

King Leopold and Queen Rabia had been away for a few days. There had been a trade meeting with Azuria that required both their attendance. They would be travelling for a number of days prior to the meeting and a number of days back. So, in their absence, Prince Thaddius would be in charge of the kingdom and all the governing that concerned it.

'You're eighteen now, son, it's high time you leaned to stand on your own two feet. The Kingdom needs strong leadership, and even though you have done well up to now, you have always had me and your mother as a safety net. For the next week or so, you will be on your own. We will be incommunicado. Every decision will be yours to stand by. Beware, though son, as you will also be accountable for your actions, and anyone else's who is acting on your behalf,' the king had told him as they sat in his chambers a few days earlier.

'Father,' Thaddius replied, his head bowed in reverence to the faith his father was putting in him. 'I will not let you down.'

Leopold smiled at him. 'I know you won't, son. You have fine Carnelian blood coursing through your veins. I know the kingdom will be safe in your hands.' His father's face then changed, and a jaunty look shone in his eyes. 'Oh, and maybe it's about time you started thinking about taking yourself a wife. Your mother and I are rather eager to become grandparents, you know,' he said, tipping his son a saucy wink. 'She must be a highborn woman, though. You can practice all you want on those low women, but the one you marry must be a Lady.' The King slapped his son on the back and walked off, chuckling to himself.

And so, it came to pass that mid-afternoon, Prince Thaddius found himself in his chambers. The curtains were drawn to keep out the light, making the room as dark as night, but there was a lot of movement playing in the shadows. The bedcovers were writhing, and small, playful, muffled squeals could be heard from beneath them. There was also a lot of laughing, and moaning.

This had been going on for some time.

The crashing open of the locked door and the sudden infusion of light into the room made all the movement beneath the covers stop, instantly. Silhouettes of heavily armed men rushing in broke that light. A head appeared out from the bed covers. The hair was dishevelled and the complexion in the newly illuminated room was ruddy. Another head popped out next to the first one, fair hair was sticking up in a thousand different angles.

Both shocked faces were sporting kiss rashes.

'What is the meaning of this?' roared an angry voice that Thaddius recognised. Endellion too. 'Get out of that bed, now, and remove that slut from his presence.'

King Leopold was furious.

'Father, it is not a slut I have in here with me,' Thaddius pleaded, sitting up, careful not to remove the covers from his guest to maintain her modesty. 'It's Lady Endellion.'

Endellion offered a small, timid smile. She knew how much the king disliked her, for what reasons, she had never been able fathom. Right now, she knew she was in trouble. Deep trouble.

'I know who it is, and I know *what* she is,' Leopold bellowed, his face flushing red with rage. 'I repeat my demand. Get that slut from beneath those blankets this instant.'

Abject terror replaced the timid smile she had been wearing moments earlier. Slowly, she wrapped the blankets around herself and climbed out of the bed. She looked at the men who had all barged in. There was no compassion on any of their faces, none of them looked at her, none, that was, except for the king himself. He looked at her as if she was something he had stepped in accidently on the street. There was nothing but utter contempt in the leer that had overtaken his features.

He reached out and ripped the blanket that covered her modesty away, leaving her standing stark naked before the seven men. She struggled to cover her modesty while the king watched. He nodded his head in mock approval. 'Yes, I can see now why she has you under her spell, Thaddius. She is indeed a beauty. But I cannot, and will not, allow this union to continue. She is lowborn and therefore not worthy of your seed.'

Thaddius was still struggling to get off the bed, untangling the bedclothes that were wrapped around him. His wide eyes shifted uneasily between his red-faced father and the even more red-faced Endellion.

'Son,' Leopold said, ignoring the naked girl. 'You are only to *dally* with this type of slut. Her kind are for practise only, that is all they are fit for. They have no concept of royalty. You do not fall in love with...' he leered at her again, his eyes slowly crawling over her nakedness, '...this!'

'Father, it's too late for that. I am in love with Endellion. She is a Lady. You yourself call her Lady Endellion.'

'I call her that as a courtesy to your mother,' the king spat as his head snapped away from Endellion's beauty, back towards his semi-naked son. 'She is no Lady. Her mother was a slut baker, cleaner, or a bar wench. Something of that ilk. She didn't even know *who* the father was. He could have been any of a thousand men that whore pleasured. Sometimes many men at a time.' Leopold's face softened a little, and most of the red that had been bursting through his veins began to dissipate. 'So, you see, my son and heir, *she* is a slut, just like her dead mother before her.'

221

Endellion could not endure any more scathes on her mother's reputation and screamed at the top of her voice. 'My mother was not a slut; she was a Lady from another realm.'

The king laughed at her outburst, and two of the men in the room put their hands on the hilts of their swords as if to stave off a likely attack. 'She was no more a Lady than I am an ostrich.'

Endellion felt rage boiling inside her, and before she knew what she was doing, she charged at the king. Her fingers flexed into dangerous claws, claws that looked like they were capable of taking an ounce of flesh. It happened so fast that it caught Leopold, Thaddius, and the rest of the men in the room off guard. She was on the King like a petrified cat, scratching at his face. Her eyes were wild, and her lips pulled back into a rictus of hate and anger.

The king, surprised by this affront on his person, fell back as the madwoman clawed at his face. 'Guards, hold her,' he wailed, his voice faltering in the middle of the shout, giving it an almost comical tint.

One of the guards stepped forward and grabbed her by her long blond hair. He heaved with an almighty effort and detached the madwoman from the king. He then threw her into the corner, where her naked body landed with a sickening crunch on a small table, shattering it into many parts.

She curled herself into a ball and began to cry.

Leopold stood up from his ordeal, his hands covering his bloodied face. He pulled them away and looked at the deep scarlet covering them.

'Seize her,' he snapped, attempting to stem the blood dripping between his fingers.

The guard who had saved him from the attack stepped forward and grabbed the weeping girl from the floor. He indicated to one of the other men in the room to pass him a sheet from off the bed, the same bed on which Prince Thaddius was sitting, watching what was happening with a lost, dazed look on his face.

'Guard, stop gawking,' the first guard snapped.

The other man removed a bed sheet and offered it to the first.

'What do you think you're doing?' the king snapped.

'I am going to wrap the Lady—'

'She is *no* Lady,' Leopold roared. 'You will leave her in the state she is. The slut should be used to being naked in the company of men.' The king smiled at his quip and turned to look at his son.

Thaddius's head was bowed. He was refusing to watch what was happening.

'Sir Ambric,' the king addressed the guard. 'As you can see, I have been assaulted. I want this lowborn whore to be paraded through the city grounds before being shackled, naked in the stocks in the centre of town. She is accused of sorcery, of seducing the prince. My son has been betrothed to Lady Halia and is to be wed within the year.' He was directing his speech more towards Thaddius and Endellion than the guard.

At the mention of his name, Thaddius looked up. A faint, pathetic smile etched onto his lips. 'Halia?' he asked, looking towards the tearful face of his lover, in the grip of the royal guard, Ambric.

'Take her away. Now,' the King hissed.

Ambric pulled the crying Endellion forwards. 'Come now, my lady,' he whispered.

From out of nowhere, she lashed out at him, raking her fingernails down his face, taking great clumps of flesh with them. He didn't seem to notice. He just adjusted his position and manoeuvred one of her arms behind her back, twisting her thumb so she was powerless to do anything but go wherever he led her.

The king, with one eye closed as blood poured into it, eyed Endellion's naked body as she was led out of the room. A wicked smile crossed his lips, one filled with lust.

Ambric marched her through the castle corridors and out towards the main halls. All of which were very busy at this time of day. 'When we get out of the view of the king,' Ambric whispered into the young girl's ear. 'I'll allow you to cover your modesty. At least until we get to the public stockades.'

'Don't do me any favours, guard,' she hissed through gritted teeth. 'We both know you'll do as your king has instructed. We also know your leader is a weak coward, a letch, and a liar. Yet you follow him blindly.'

Ambric exhaled deeply through his nostrils. 'I follow him because he's my king. Regardless of his traits. I am his subject.'

She fell silent then, a poor frightened girl who had just found herself in the worst possible situation one could find themselves in. She was angry, humiliated, scared. 'Please, Sir Ambric, let me go,' she suddenly pleaded. 'I'll disappear. Nobody will ever see me again. You could say I tricked you with my evil sorcery. No one would be any wiser.' Her voice was sobbing as she whispered her plea.

Ambric stoically marched her on through the corridor. 'I cannot, my lady. I am duty bound to carry out my orders.'

He continued his march through the castle, parading her naked through the corridors, hallways, and great rooms. To his credit, Ambric attempted to conceal her vulnerability from the castle, taking her on routes he knew were seldom trod by the populous, and wrapped her in his cloak when he could. People she had known all her life watched as she was frogmarched past them. Some were shocked, others showed pity, but most of them laughed and pointed. All of them turned their faces as she pleaded for help. One or two who attempted to intervene were parried away, in no uncertain terms, by Ambric, who told them this punishment was a direct order of the king.

He continued to lead her the quickest way through the castle, ensuring her visibility was at a minimum.

Finally, they reached the public stockades in the centre of the city. There were three stocks lined up next to each other, all currently empty. Ambric guided her into the middle one. He forced her hands and neck into the grooves. She didn't put up any fight as he closed the top over her.

She was naked and sore from the march, she was bent over into the stocks, but most of all, she was utterly humiliated.

She closed her eyes. 'How can it be that I go from a fantastic morning in bed with my prince to this within an hour? Sir Ambric, please tell me, where is Thaddius? Why has he not come to rescue me?'

Ambric was silent as people began to line up in the street to see what the fuss was about. As per his orders, he hung a sign over her head, allowing it to swing from her neck. It read:

I AM A WHORE AND A WITCH.

I SECUCED A MEMBER OF THE

ROYAL FAMILY.

I AM DISPLAYED HERE FOR YOUR

AMUSMENT.

The good people of Carnelia ogled her nakedness. The crowd was made up mostly of men who held glasses of mead, or beer in their hands. She did not think her chances of survival through the night in this atmosphere, were good.

As the day passed, people came and went. Some of the men, and even the younger boys, gave her unwarranted attention. Women and girls spat on her. She had even been urinated on by a cheering gang of youths, none of them any older than herself.

That was during the day.

She dreaded what might happen to her during the darker hours.

Eventually, night came, and with it, the cold, the hunger, and, worst of all, the thirst. Mercifully, at least, most residents had left the streets for the comforts of their homes and beds.

Endellion envied them that.

When she was alone, a heavy melancholy enveloped her, and it was then the tears came for real. *Where is Thaddius?* she wept. *Was it only this morning he professed his undying love for me? Was he just using me?* She didn't think that had been the case. They had known each other for years, had grown up together. *He does love me ... doesn't he?*

With those thoughts teasing her, stoking her paranoia, she lolled into an uneasy sleep. A sleep where she couldn't move and was freezing cold.

~~~~

The next morning, Endellion was awoken with a bucket of warm liquid thrown over her. The warmth comforted her as she snapped from a horrible dream, until she realised what it was. As the stinking urine dripped from her hair and face, she watched the old hag who had done it walk away cackling loudly. She simply watched her go. She had nothing left inside her, no energy to scream, to curse her, there were no tears to cry; all that was left was an intense hatred. She hated the old hag; she hated the men who had touched her in places she'd only allowed Thaddius to see. She hated everyone who had seen her paraded through the castle. She hated Sir Ambric; she hated the queen and the king. But most of all, she hated Thaddius.

How could my love allow this to happen to me?

Tears were hard to come by.

No moisture had fallen since her attack of melancholy the night before. Even as the taste of the old woman's waste seeped into her throat and dripped from her nose, she could not cry.

I won't cry. It's what they want. They want to see me break down; they want me to cry, yell, and scream for mercy. To admit to sorcery or whatever they've accused me of. But I won't, I won't ... I WON'T!'

The day dragged. Her back screamed in agony; she had been bent into the same position for almost twenty-four hours. Hunger had taken its toll, and thirst was now also taking a grip. Shame, well that had been and gone. It had taken off right after the first time she'd had to defecate. She'd held it in for as long as she could, but in the end, nature had taken its course and she had to let it go. A group of school children were present when it happened, and their screams and laughter hurt, not only her ears.

That precise moment had been the turning point for her. She vowed if she were to escape this predicament, she would have vengeance on the king, the queen, and ... a solitary tear ran down her face when she thought of him, but she wouldn't allow it to take a grip on her ... Prince Thaddius.

In fact, she thought with a venomous spite, *the whole Kingdom of Carnelia will feel my wrath.*

An old man shuffled up to her. As he got closer, she could smell the stench of stale alcohol and a vinegar stink of dirt and sweat ingrained into his body and clothes. As he looked at her, he licked his dry, cracked lips. She clenched her fists as she braced herself for the inevitable feel of his dirty hands fondling her in public. She waited for him to use her in whatever way he saw fit. She knew no one would stop him and thought the populace may even encourage him. He licked his lips again before reaching into a pocket in the front of his tunic. She didn't want to look but couldn't tear her eyes away from the old wretch.

He produced a broken cob of bread. He held it out to her in his filthy hands.

Now the sting of tears came; tears she had vowed would not fall, welled in her eyes. The man's generosity was new to her, and she ate the stale bread, thankfully, as he snapped off small bits and fed them to her. It was stale, mouldy … and fantastic.

'Thank you,' she croaked.

The man didn't answer, he just smiled, licked his lips again, and shuffled off in the direction he had come.

That was the only highpoint of what she would think back upon, and mark, as the lowest point in her life. She promised herself that the man's kindness would not blight her vision of revenge on this stinking kingdom.

She had been abused and laughed at, but what she didn't know was all she had endured would only act as a prelude to her ultimate disgrace.

This came roughly one hour after sundown. The streets had cleared as most of the populace would be home, cooking, eating, enjoying their lives. She had resigned herself to death that night, either from exposure or someone being overzealous with the abuse she had been receiving.

That was then King Leopold strolled by.

He walked along the street, arm in arm with Queen Rabia.

As they passed, they looked at her. The first thing she noticed about the king was the eye patch he was sporting, presumably from where she'd scratched him. The second was the contempt in his good eye, for her, along with the smug satisfaction of his smile as he regarded her in the stocks. In the queen's face, she thought—or hoped—she saw pity and sorrow. However, the woman who had professed to be her friend, her surrogate mother, her protector, did nothing but stand with her husband and look at her.

The worst moment came seconds later from this indignity. It happened when Thaddius appeared behind them. Initially, her heart leapt when she saw him. *My prince, he's come to rescue me,* she thought. Confusion nestled in the creases of her face as she saw the young lady on his arm. Endellion had seen her around the castle before. It was Lady Halia, the daughter of a courtier of the king and queen.

The couple walked past Endellion, and as they did, the young prince didn't once look at her.

Even after everything that had happened, this was still the worst moment. Her heart broke. It shattered into a million pieces. All her mighty efforts came to nothing at this moment, and the tears that had been threatening, finally flowed. There was nothing she could do to hold them back.

Thaddius caught up with his father. 'She knew I was vulnerable, as you and Mother were not home. She used her witchcraft to seduce me.

230

She used my royal body as a plaything.' Thaddius refused to make eye contact with her, and Endellion could see Lady Halia looking at her with disgust and contempt.

Thankfully, they didn't stay long. It seemed that they quickly bored of the spectacle of her humiliation, and the four of them wandered off, led by King Leopold. Only Rabia and Thaddius looked back.

She thought, or maybe hoped, there was concern, maybe even regret in their eyes.

She bit her tongue until they were gone. There was no way she would give that bastard Leopold any satisfaction. She waited, and waited until they, and their entourage, had passed out of sight before her dam broke. Thick tears streamed down her cheeks like they had never flowed before. A guttural scream fled from her mouth. It had issued from her stomach, but it felt like it had been her soul. Her life had been spent around those people. They had raised her, treated her as one of their own. She loved them as her family. She loved one of them differently than the others. Loved him with all her heart. It was an emotional, and physical love.

She knew he had loved her too. He had told her on many occasions.

Now, they were all strangers.

To watch them turn their backs on her while she stood naked and humiliated, chained to stocks for the whole of the kingdom to see, was too much for her to bear.

She no longer wished revenge on them; she now wished that *she* were dead. She wished she had died with her mother eighteen years ago.

As the day's humiliation drew on, she didn't think it could get any worse.

She was wrong.

~~~~~

Soon the dark and the cold of the night began to bite her. The streets were again deserted, and she was alone. The tears from earlier had not stopped, and she worried about how much hydration they were using. *Am I to be left here until I die?* The terror of that thought pushed her, momentarily to forget the biting cold, the gnawing hunger, and her blistering thirst.

The world around her blurred as her vision began to darken. Her frazzled mind recognised the oncoming of death, and strangely welcoming it. There was even a warmth to it, a fuzz like the world was turning … purple!

A flurry of noise snapped her from her malaise. Four men approached from the gloom; two were carrying lamps and broadswords. For an instant, her heart sang as she thought she was about to be released.

Maybe Thaddius has come for me at last.

Her elation was short-lived as she recognised the men.

At first, she saw them as just Royal Guards, here to have fun at her expense. She had been abused so much in the last two days that she no longer cared what happened to her, or who did it. However, as the first guard stepped up, she recognised him.

Her heart dropped into her stomach, and odd as it seemed, given her thoughts of less than five minutes earlier, she feared for her life.

There was a gauze over the soldier's cheek. It was where she'd scratched him. The moment she saw it, she recognised him as Ambric. If he was here, then she knew he would be guarding someone important.

She hoped it was Thaddius, but something told her, her luck would not permit it.

In a moment, she was proved right. Another man stepped out from behind him, this one was dressed in common clothing, but it was a terrible disguise.

It was King Leopold.

She closed her eyes, trying not to imagine the terrible abuses he was here to administer. She was numb from her head to her feet; but it wasn't just a physical numbness, it was emotional too. There was another man behind the king; he was also dressed in commoner clothing, but he looked more than uncomfortable being here.

Her bad luck, it seemed, held no bounds.

Oh Glimm, no ... please don't let that be Thaddius. But no matter how much she pleaded with the Great Lord Glimm, or to any other Gods, none could deny the fact that it *was* Thaddius. Her only true love, the man she had willingly given herself to, had come to mock her.

King Leopold removed the hat he was wearing as part of his pathetic disguise. With a drunken leer, he bent down and looked her in the face. She winced as his foul breath, stinking of stale alcohol and fish, breathed into her face. 'Well now, my little common whore, I think it's time you were dealt your real punishment. Eh?' he slurred.

She was relieved when he removed his face, but her relief was not long lived.

He also removed his tunic, and she saw he was naked beneath, naked and excited. He moved around to the back of her.

She was helpless to resist, all she could do was close her eyes, and think about happier time, as the king, the protector of the realm, the *just* King Leopold, raped her.

He took her, satisfying his carnal lusts before his guards and his son, the man she loved. As it happened, she opened her eyes and looked at the three remaining men. The one guard she didn't recognise was enjoying the king's show, grinning and nudging the others. Ambric and Thaddius were looking away. Neither able to watch, yet, she noted, neither of them doing anything to help.

As her ordeal passed, she continued to look at them. Forcing them to acknowledge her, and what had just happened. From face to face she vowed, from the lowest, darkest parts of being, that she would kill them.

In this world, or in the next. It matters not to me ...

'Come now, my fine fellows,' Leopold chuckled drunkenly. 'This is what she's here for. Our enjoyment,' he shouted gleefully as he mocked her. 'You, Thaddius, surely, you'll want one more ride on this fine whore before you marry your pretty, highborn wife?'

Thaddius, to his credit, didn't answer.

'No? Ah well, your loss, my boy. But then, I believe you've had everything you want from this slut anyway. 'How about you Ambric. A fine soldier like you must need to relieve some of his stress, from time to time, eh?'

Ambric bowed his head. 'I will have to pass on this offer, my liege,' he mumbled.

'I'll have a go,' the second soldier shouted, and pushed past Ambric, almost knocking him in his eager rush. Ambric grabbed him and stared hard into his face.

The man, the soldier shrugged him off. He looked to the king, who was now clapping, edging him on.

Endellion endured a second, shameful attack. When he was finished, he hooted into the night.

'Come then,' the king shouted. 'We've had our fill of this whore, let us find ourselves more mead and celebrate this young man's engagement.'

As they walked away, she heard the king roar with laughter and slap his son on the back.

Her tears stopped, and they did not return.

She was bruised, sore, used, and humiliated, but now she was mostly apathetic. She no longer cared about anything. She was empty. She was trapped in the stocks, naked, raped, humiliated, freezing, and ready to die.

She laughed.

She laughed for a long time. How long, she couldn't tell, but her ribs were sore by the end of it.

Tears of humourless mirth clouded her vision. Within the blur, she noticed a purple hue forming. She thought it odd, as there had not been a return of the purple lady for many years. *Maybe she's come to guide me through to the other side, s*he thought. *Or maybe I'm seeing things.*

Closing her eyes brought sweet relief from the madness that was settling into her brain, but when she opened them again, the purple lady, the same one from her youth, was standing, or more precisely hovering, before her.

The woman had not changed, or aged, since she'd seen her last, maybe ten years earlier.

The lady smiled down at her, and with a click of her fingers, the stocks around Endellion's neck and hands unlocked.

She could not believe what was happening, but the pins and needles in her hands, as the blood rushed back into them, told her this was not a dream.

'Am I dead?' she asked as she stood upright, wincing as her back and neck protested. She looked back, expecting to see her lifeless body hanging in the stocks and that she was now a ghost. But they were empty.

Shaking her wrists and rubbing her neck, she eyed the purple woman. *She looks like me*, she thought.

With that thought still lingering in her head, she watched as the woman moved away; turning only once to beckon her to follow her.

She did.

The purple spectre led her through the city, taking her down lesser known, quieter alleyways and dark, shadowy streets. Endellion had never seen this side of the city. She marvelled at the way these people lived, among squalor and filth. She wondered why her purple guide was showing her this way but soon realised that she was making sure her passage through the kingdom was as secretive as possible. The woman led her down an alleyway where clothing was hanging on a line to dry. Endellion found something that fit her, to a fashion, and wrapped the garments around her, relishing the warmth they offered.

Soon after, they came upon the castle from a direction she had never seen before. The purple woman pointed towards a small hatch in the wall, and Endellion opened it. As she climbed in, she was surprised to find herself in the kitchens.

After allowing her to quench her thirst and satiate her hunger, the ghostly woman led her on a merry dance through rooms and corridors she did not even know existed. Then they came upon a corridor that Endellion did know, very well. It was the one that led to the jewel room.

The purple woman hovered over the trapdoor, illuminating it in the darkness, and Endellion entered the gloom below.

The darkness was deep, but she knew from memory how many steps there were to the other corridor. She knew how far it was to the door the woman intended her to enter.

The door was open, as she knew it would be.

She pushed it wide; the purple glow informed her that the lady was already inside. The glow from her presence did not reflect on the many jewels inside, it seemed strange to her, but not something to dwell upon.

The woman indicated towards the array of priceless jewels that were lying around the room, and Endellion, not needing to be told twice, filled her pockets with them. Her ghostly guide then hovered over the unremarkable box that Endellion knew contained the small ball, the one she had been drawn to so many times in the past. Her guide gave this more credence than anything else in the room, so Endellion took it.

The moment she removed it, it began to glow red.

'Thank you, Endellion,' the lady said.

Endellion dropped the ball and stepped back, away from the ghost. She had never, not once in any of their meetings, spoken.

The lady smiled and pointed to the ball again. Endellion, not taking her eyes from the spectre, bent and picked it up. Instantly, it regained its deep glowing red.

The lady spoke again.

Her voice was soft and low, but most of all, it was kind. It was the first kindly voice she had heard in what felt like years. 'There now, we can communicate. You are probably wondering who I am and why I'm here. I am a Sister of the Purple. My powers are confined to the walls of this castle and city. I have been your guide through your life, and I am here now to guide you once again through this most difficult transition. Endellion, it is time you left this place. You need to go now and take the Glimmer with you. It will protect you. You should study it and learn its power.'

'Glimmer?' Endellion asked, confusion carved through the grimace on her illuminated face.

'The ball you hold. It is a Glimmer. It is the source of great power. It is now yours to command,' the lady said.

'Are … you my mother?' Endellion asked, not sure if she wanted to know. It just seemed like the correct question to ask.

The spectre smiled. 'No, my child. I'm not, I am a Sister of the Purple, as was your mother. That makes me honour bound to help you all I can. The Glimmer that you possess is powerful. You should use it with caution and with responsibility. I must leave you now. I am honour bound to avenge your wrongdoing. Leave this place Endellion, leave it now and never, ever come back.'

'How do I leave without being seen?'

'You already know a way out of the city, child. Use it and heed my words. Never come back.'

The vision of the woman disappeared, leaving Endellion alone in the jewel filled room, illuminated by the red orb in her hands. She put it into a deep pocket and then set out to find the trap door to her freedom.

It took her a while, as her head was filled with all the purple ghost had told her, but eventually, she located the trapdoor and made her way out. As she traversed the ancient throne room with its wicker seat in the centre, she felt the ball— *the Glimmer?* —in her pocket vibrate.

She looked for the old drawings that depicted the journey of the old man all those thousands of years ago and memorised them. Within an hour, she was exiting a tunnel into a vast expanse of open air. She needed somewhere to rest; daylight was breaking around her, and she only wanted to travel under cover of night. She gripped the Glimmer in her pocket and closed her eyes. A route revealed itself to her then. A purple path leading towards an old shelter, where she lay down and slept the whole day away.

~~~

The next morning, the castle was alive with activity. An urgent buzz was passing between the villagers. Something was afoot. Castle guards were running around the city, fully armed, bursting into the homes of known trouble causers and villains. These homes were then ransacked before the homeowners were marched off towards the castle. It was clear they were looking for something, or someone.

Prince Thaddius and Queen Rabia had been roused early from their slumbers. Still confused with sleep, they had been bid to follow the contingency of guards.

'Where is my husband?' Queen Rabia demanded as she and her son were harried through the castle, surrounded on every side by armed soldiers.

As they passed through the city, their subjects stopped what they were doing, removed their headgear, and bowed their heads towards the royal couple.

'What is happening?' the queen demanded again.

'Yes, man. Explain this. What is happening, and where is my father?'

The guard in charge of their escort was Sir Ambric. 'All will be revealed very soon, My Liege,' he replied.

Thaddius had detected a sombre tone to the words, and he stared, a little too long, at the young guard. 'I am not your Liege, Ambric. My father is. Now, I demand you tell me what is hap—'

Thaddius never finished his sentence.

As they rounded a corner, they ran into a large crowd of onlookers. Prince Thaddius noted they were in the city square. The crowd had gathered, staring at something in the vicinity of the stocks.

Thaddius's heart sank.

He imagined the worst for poor Endellion.

But what he saw shocked him even more.

It was not his beloved Endellion in the stocks.

He had expected to see her limp, dirty, naked body, and he had expected to be heartbroken. But instead of young pink flesh, there was a large pudgy body. It was that of a much older person, and it was a man. It took Thaddius a moment to recognise who it was slumped and naked in the centre of the courtyard.

It was his father.

King Leopold.

His plump body had been forced into the stocks, but whoever had the audacity to do this to the king had not bothered to lock them. The expression on his lifeless face was fear. His dead eyes were wide open, bulging, as they stared into the great abyss, forever petrified by whatever, or whoever could do something like this to a king. His mouth hung open as his bloated tongue lolled from his purple lips. A dark puddle of blood lay congealing on the floor beneath him. Thaddius looked up from the puddle and noticed that it dripped from the deep slash in his father's flabby neck.

Ambric had been right when he called him *My Liege.*

Thaddius was now King of Carnelia.

He immediately took charge of the situation. 'You there, and you there,' he shouted, gesturing towards members of the Royal Guard dotted about the crowd. 'Get my father's body away from here and cover his modesty for the sake of the kingdom.'

The men snapped to attention and began to work on the task at hand.

10.

ENDELLION, NOW YEARS older and infinitely wiser, sat on the wicker throne beneath the castle of Carnelia, or as it was now known, The City of the Fireflies.

She was home.

At long last!

Part 5

1.

IT HAD BEEN nearly a week since they'd had word of the attack on the Rebel's camp, and Bernard and Cass were worried. In that time, there had been no communication from Ambric and his team. There were a lot of frustrated and worried men within the boundaries of the fortress that was Outpost Three.

'We have to go and find them,' Cassandra argued vehemently to the men sat around the table, in the room they had come to know as the war room. 'At the very least, we should outstretch our resources towards them.'

'We've sent several search parties already. If we send any more, it will weaken our position here,' was the response from one of the men.

'Our position is already precarious at best. We're holed up in one stronghold. It is a good position to be in, but at any time, the Azurians could offer up a siege, and we'd be stuck. We have limited resources, and the grounds of this outpost are not exactly what you would call fertile,' Bernard countered. 'If we don't begin to spread ourselves out, then we're already doomed. Ambric is a resourceful man, one of Carnelia's best. He may well have found another defendable outpost that we can link our defences to. It's my opinion that we need to find him and his team.'

'I agree,' came another shout from the room. Matthew stood, getting the attention of everyone. 'We need Ambric, and his numbers. By now, there's no question they know we hold this encampment. I'm amazed they haven't already sent a vanguard to engage us. Yes, we grow in strength every day, but what do we really have? We have us, plus what might be left of the Rebels. What is that against the might of an entire kingdom?' He sat down again, resting his elbows on the table and shaking his head. 'I do *not* fancy that fight,' he concluded.

'I'm in agreement with Matthew. We need an advanced search party,' Bernard spoke over the growing murmurs. 'All those in favour, raise your hands.'

He counted a lot more hands than he was expecting. 'And those against ...' A few men raised their arms, but the decision was a clear one. 'Right then. The decision is final. As per Matthew's suggestion, we will set up a search party and go looking for Ambric and his men at first light.'

'I should be on that search party,' Cassandra shouted over the noise of the room. Her statement caused a hush to descend. Every eye fell upon her. Her face flushed at the attention, but she carried on regardless. 'It

245

makes sense. I know the terrain, I know how the Azurians work, and I look like their queen.' She smiled and shook her head at her last statement. 'Actually, I am their queen,' she continued. A light laughter filtered through the room. 'However, there's still an issue that needs to be addressed.'

'What is it, Cass?' Bernard asked.

She looked around her. She didn't believe that none of them could see the glaring problem with her not only being on the search party but with her being in the Ferals in the first instance.

'Are you going to tell us, girl, or make us play twenty questions?' piped a voice from the back of the room.

'Do all of you have such short memories? Do none of you remember how we took this castle in the first instance?' She looked around the room and was astonished at the blank faces. 'I *am* the Queen of Azuria,' she said, gesturing around the room, pausing, waiting for the penny to drop.

It didn't.

Men, she tutted, rolling her eyes in their sockets. 'Well, their queen isn't me, but she does look like me.'

Again, there were blank faces.

'Do I need to spell this out for you? We took this castle by tricking the Azurian Guard into thinking I was the woman impersonating me. What's to stop them from performing the same trick on us?'

The penny finally dropped. The men looked at each other and nodded, as if to say they knew what she was talking about all along and were just waiting for someone else to mention it.

'We're going to need codes, or something. Something they would never be able to guess. So if I turn back up at the castle and I don't know the code, then don't let me in.' She addressed the group in a manner akin to a schoolmistress teaching her subjects.

'And then we kill her,' shouted another voice. This one was followed carefully by a chorus of approval from almost everyone in the room.

Cassandra was the only one who didn't approve.

~~~~

By early morning, a code had been agreed and the search and rescue team had been picked. They were fully equipped and ready to deploy. Their first destination was the last known location of Ambric's Rebels.

Cassandra was dressed, armoured, and ready to go.

'It is over a day's ride from here. Everyone is rested, and we have the best of the Azurian horses. They have been well fed and watered. We're all set. Remember…' Bernard directed this to the guard on the walls. '…if Cass, on her return, does not know what the code is, then we do not allow her inside. Understood?'

The mounted guard nodded his understanding.

'Then we'll have your leave.' Bernard raised his sword and shouted before galloping through the open portcullis and away from the outpost. He was followed closely by a band of eighteen men and one woman.

2.

ENDELLION WAS IN her chambers. She had been too preoccupied with her own adventures and musings to notice what was happening around the castle. In truth, she had no interest in what else was happening other than her own vengeance and lust for power. She had reverted to her own image to make passing through the castle easier, to avoid anyone asking her if she was OK or trying to guide her in any way. No one would give any notice to an old woman making her way through the corridors in the course of her duties, whatever they may be.

At one point in her journey back from the ancient throne, Alexander had marched past with a group of men. He was barking orders and directing them around the castle. Without thinking, she hailed him as they passed. 'Hello, Alexander…' she said before walking on.

The youth stopped and looked at her. His face changed as recollection dawned. He cocked his head and shouted. 'Stop right there, old woman.'

Endellion, realising the slip she had just made, cursed under her breath. With her eyes closed she stopped and turned towards him, bowing low. 'Yes, my prince?'

'I know you,' he stated. 'I've seen you before. Where do I know you from?'

Endellion's face was one of utter innocence, her eyes wide and her lips pouted. 'I do not know, my lord. I'm a serving maid for your sister, the queen. Mayhap you've seen me bringing food and drawing baths.'

'No, that's not it.' He turned away and consulted his men for a short moment. Endellion took the chance to slip her hand into her pocket and wrap her fingers around the Glimmer concealed inside. She closed her eyes and her face altered slightly. Not by much, but enough to hopefully confuse the boy, and allow her to leave.

He turned back. 'No, I've definitely met you before …' He then took another, closer look into her face. His eyes squinted before he waved her away, impatiently. 'I can't remember where. It can't be important. Go and draw my sister her bath. Tell her I will be seeking her counsel later.'

'Yes, my lord. I'll let her know.'

'Oh, and next time …'

Endellion turned back towards the prince. 'Yes?'

'Next time you see me, do not be so familiar. I am your prince, and you will address me as such.'

Endellion bowed and curtseyed, and then was off. She continued to curse inwardly at another stupid mistake. *That's the third time I've let that happen. Stupid, stupid mistake. If he were to put it together that he had seen me at Azuria, at the encampment, and then here, there would be trouble. If he ever makes that connection, then the young, brave Alexander will be having a little ... accident!*

The rest of the journey to her chambers was uneventful. She ducked into a small empty room as she got closer to change back into Casandra's image, and the guards allowed her into her room.

Once the door was locked, she sat in the centre of a rug and removed the Glimmer from its folds. As it began to glow, she found herself back in the ancient throne room. Her guide was waiting for her, smiling as he always did.

'Who are the Sisters of the Purple?' she asked without any niceties.

With a satisfied grin, she watched her guide's smile falter, then fall.

'Tell me, old man, who are the Sisters of the Purple? I do not want any of your cryptic answers either. I want a straight answer for once. Who are the Sisters of the Purple?'

The old man was silent for a while. She could see his mouth moving beneath his beard as he contemplated the question. Eventually, he turned away and looked like he was conversing with someone she couldn't see.

After a short while, he turned back and took a deep breath. 'The Sisters of the Purple are a strong, proud people. In the bygone days when our race was also strong and proud, it was decided that only the most intelligent and dedicated boys would be allowed to become a Brother of the Glimm, entering into our hierarchy. It was a silly and misogynistic decision, based on nothing other than pride and elitism. There had never been a female allowed into the ranks of the Glimm. That was a ridiculous decision, one that eventually caused the destruction of our kind.'

Endellion interjected his story with a small chuff.

The Glimm guide flashed a stern look before continuing.

'The females were, in some cases, stronger mentally than the men, and through the years, it was speculated they were ostracised from the Glimm for being *too* strong. The male hierarchy were threatened by them somehow. They were not allowed in the temples and were left to run the villages, to bring up the children. These women began their own sect. They called themselves the Sisters of the Purple. There is still evidence of their sect, even now, although they are nowhere near as powerful as they once were. Mostly, all they have now is latent genes and old manuscripts to dwell over. There are also several ghosts. They are powerful, but ghosts nonetheless.'

'Are they allies to the Glimm?'

The guide blinked and momentarily and turned away again. 'They only look after their own, and only in times of severity.'

'Like me being held in the stocks in Carnelia?' she asked.

'Exactly.' The Glimm nodded.

'Would they be able to help me find the Throne of Glimm? If you won't, maybe they will ...'

Her guide let out a deep sigh, he shook his head slowly. 'Always with the Throne with you. No, I don't think they could help. And the way you abuse your Glimmer, I don't suppose they would *want* to help.'

Endellion smiled a sly grin. Her eyes narrowed and darkened. 'Well then, it's a good job that I've found it myself then, isn't it?'

The Glimm's face fell again. His eyes grew wide as his features elongated beneath his beard. 'You have?' he asked.

'Yes,' Endellion laughed. 'And all from my own devices too.' Before she opened her eyes in her chambers, removing herself from the Alter, she had the gratification of seeing a look of panic on her guide's, otherwise gentle, face.

~~~

Feeling good after her confrontation with the Glimm, Endellion decided it was time for bed. She would need all her energy for the trip to the Throne room. It would be this that sealed her destiny and allowed her to achieve the true power she craved and deserved.

Dog tired, she was just about to climb under the covers when a knock on the door disturbed her. She sighed, closed her eyes, and decided to ignore it, assuming whoever it was would go away. She continued into bed. The moment before she pulled the blankets over her, to embrace the long awaited and required sleep, the knock came again. This time it was more urgent than the last.

'Sister! Are you there?' It was Alexander, half whispering, half shouting from the other side of the door.

She growled at the sound of his voice. As she had released herself back to her own form earlier, she flicked her blankets back and grasped the Glimmer at the side of her bed. The wind formed in the room and changed back in her back into Cassandra's image. Wrapping herself in a robe, she hurried towards the door. 'I'm coming, my brother, stay patient.'

As she opened it, she was greeted with a very excited youth. 'Did your maid servant inform you I needed your counsel?'

'Yes, she did. I waited for you, but I'm tired now, brother. Can it not wait until the morning?'

Alexander smiled. Endellion noted there was very little humour in it; this made her a little bit happier. 'No, sister, it can't. We have them!'

'Who?' she asked, only half interested. All thoughts and motivations had been concentrated on finding the Altar of Glimm, she had given little thought to issues of the realm.

'The Rebels. We have them, and the Ferals too. All of them, in one swoop.'

Suddenly he had her full attention. The news piqued her interest. This could be the chance she needed to rid herself of any resistance to her ultimate plan. 'Is the intelligence reliable?' she snapped, suddenly awake.

'Completely, my queen. I've had men scout Outpost Three since we've been back. They have tracked a pack of riders towards the last known location of the Rebels, the very same that we bettered with our fireflies. Our men are in sight of them as we speak. We're watching and waiting for them to find each other. Once they do, we'll take them all in one swift motion.'

This was music to Endellion's ears. She could feel her heart thudding after every word. 'Excellent work, my brother,' she congratulated him, noting that his excited smile stretched just that little bit further, almost ear to ear. 'Do we need to ride tonight?'

Alexander shook his head. 'No. We'll have time enough to leave at first light.'

'Good,' Endellion replied. 'Then, please allow me let me catch up on my sleep so I can be fresh for our ride. Goodnight, sweet brother. And once again, good work.'

'Goodnight, my queen,' he whispered.

As the door closed, he straightened his tunic and checked his weapon. Once satisfied, he walked off in the direction of the main officers' mess with the air of a man with great purpose.

3.

AS SHE WOKE, Endellion had a good feeling. *Today is the day. Everything I've wished and worked for will come to fruition today. I'll have the Rebels in my grip, and I'll travel to the Throne of Glimm to take my rightful place as the most powerful being in this world.*

She was beaming as she prepared for the long ride.

Arriving in the courtyard, she was running slightly late, but she knew no one was going to chide their queen about punctuality. Her fireflies were everywhere. At first, she hardly noticed them, what with everything else going on in her head, but when she did, she saw they were very prominent indeed. 'Alexander, please tell me why the fireflies are in such attendance.'

'Well,' he began, his huge grin still on his face from the night before, 'since you gave me control over them, I thought we could use them to fortify the kingdom. To make it impenetrable. To truly make it The City of the Fireflies.'

'You have exceeded yourself, brother. Not only are you a Knight of the Realm, the Queen's personal protector, it would seem you are now a custodian of this great kingdom. Mayhap I should watch myself around you, Alex. You might have ideas regarding my crown.'

The boy laughed, he also blushed in a boyish way. It was the blush that bothered her more than anything else. She laughed as she watched him walk away. 'I'm not laughing inside, brat. Maybe I *will* watch you, and closely!'

4.

AS THE BAND of twenty, including Bernard and Cassandra, reached what had been the last known camp of Ambric and his Rebels, it was already growing dark. The men and horses were exhausted from the long journey.

'We should make up camp here for the night,' Bernard said as he dismounted his steed. 'I would guess Ambric has entered a tunnel network. I can't see him making camp with no clear way to escape an attack. If we know what to look for, then they should be rather straightforward to find. Luckily, I have trained with Ambric, and have grown to understand his ways. We'll locate and enter the tunnels at first light. I for one don't fancy a journey into the unknown tonight.'

The entourage dismounted and continued with the erection of a make-shift camp, including an impromptu cooking area and latrines. Two of the men took themselves into the surrounding forest to hunt rabbit, or anything else, to complement their rations. They returned twenty minutes later with a string of prey tied around each of their shoulders. The offerings were swiftly skinned, prepared, and cooked. A decent meal was had by all.

Then it was time for goodnights, and everyone trailed off to their tents with the understanding of an early rise in the morning.

Bernard and Cassandra had called first watch and were huddled together, keeping warm by the fire.

'What do you think we'll find down there?' she asked, trying to make conversation to take her thoughts away from the fact that the man she had fallen in love with was sitting next to her and they were alone before a roaring fire in the middle of nowhere.

Bernard shook his head and poked the flames with a stick. The fire didn't need poking, but he did it anyway. 'I don't know, to be honest. This isn't somewhere Ambric would take his cadets. Although I know there are places like this dotted around the countryside. I'm as new to all this as you are. Could you not ask your, your ...'—she could see he was struggling to remember the name of her Glimmer—'...your thing, you know, to find out where they are?'

She laughed at his nervousness, mostly because she felt it too. The smell of the fire and the damp trees around them, plus the swooshing of the wind breezing through the leaves in the night, was having an effect on her as well. 'Do you know what? I haven't even thought about that. My guide told me I have access to a plethora of their talents. I've been trying to use remote sight but have only had limited success, up until now.'

She excused herself on the pretence of going to the toilet and entered the woods. She dug deep into her pocket and produced the Glimmer, then closed her eyes. No sooner were they closed than the orb began to glow a deep blue. Cassandra became motionless. It looked like she was not there anymore, as if her essence had moved on somewhere else, leaving her body in waiting for her to come back.

In the Altar room, her guide was smiling and waiting patiently for her. 'How may I be of help, my child?' he asked in his kindly way.

'I need the ability of remote sight.'

'Ah, a difficult skill, that is. But it is one a person with your abilities should be able to master with little effort.'

Cassandra smiled at his encouragement. 'I have used it before, but I need it tonight. Well, right now, actually,' she continued.

The Glimm laughed, a deep and resonant sound echoing around the chamber. 'You already have it, child. From the moment you used it the first time, it became yours. Now all I need to do is instruct you on how to hone the talent.'

Her Glimm guide sat on the floor and Cassandra sat next to him. His eyes were closed, as were hers. 'I want you to picture a face. The face of the person you want to remotely see. You need to think of every detail of this face. How their nose looks, what colour their eyes are, do they have any facial scars.'

Cassandra thought about the last time she had seen Ambric. She didn't really know him that well and tried her best to get the details of his features correct. 'His nose is thin and pointed, and I think his eyes are brown. I remember that he has three old but deep-looking scars down his face, over one of his eyes.'

'Good, good. Now keep that image with you. Do you see it?'

Cassandra nodded. She did see Ambric.

'Now, what colour is his hair? His eyebrows? How broad are his shoulders? Does he have a beard? Keep all of these thoughts with you and concentrate on them.'

There was a flash of colour in the darkness behind her eyelids. It was red. It looked like it could have been Ambric's armour, although the flash was far too fast for her to make anything of.

Then there was another flash.

It looked like a room, a dark and dimly lit room. Men were sitting around it.

Then there was a third flash.

This time a large area opened up before her closed eyes. It was a campsite. There was a fire in the centre. Sitting around the fire was …

'Yes, yes, you see. You're working it. The remote viewing is coming to you,' her guide gushed. 'Can you focus on anything? Anything with detail?'

Another flash came to her.

This time she knew it was Ambric's armour she was seeing. He was wearing it as he sat at a makeshift table with his back against a wall. She knew, deep down, she could find this location.

'Can I take this talent out into my world?' she asked, knowing that sometimes it was harder to do things in the real world than it was to do them in this chamber. The butterflies were a prime example.

'I do not see why not,' her guide replied with a smile.

Did he just make a joke? she thought but didn't want to ask in case it offended him.

'You're growing in power and strength every day. Go, see if you can take this with you. It is yours to take.' He made a shooing gesture towards her but kept his smile

'Thank you,' she said, and opened her eyes.

As they opened into her own world, she was surprised to see it was almost light. She wanted to test her ability for remote sight in this world as soon as she could, so she grabbed her Glimmer and concentrated on Ambric, his face, and his armour.

The image came to her instantly. He was sleeping on a stack of what looked like rags, using them as a makeshift bed. Instinctively, she knew where he, and his Rebels were and, more importantly, how she could find them. With an air of excitement, she dashed from the woods; only for her feeling of elation to be ripped from her. Her smile quickly turned into a frown of horror, sorrow, and distaste.

When they had arrived at camp, it was dark, and the first thing that needed to be done was to build a fire to cook their evening meal. The darkness and the smell of the roasting meat masked something else, something sinister. Glancing around, the horror of the scene dawned on her slowly. The men were at work, either digging or dragging sacks along

261

the floor. Only on closer inspection did she realise they were not just sacks.

They were corpses.

They had inadvertently built their camp to the side of the entrance of the tunnels they had been looking for, the very centre of the attack that forced Ambric and his men into hiding. Obviously, they had run into the cover at haste and not had time to return to honour their dead.

Bernard's men were doing that duty for them now.

Cassandra was shocked and horrified as she counted the numbers of the dead. Most had been torn apart, others appeared to have been impaled. The scene was horribly similar to the battle she witnessed at the beginning all this madness. The battle where she had been captured and imprisoned by Endellion and her fireflies.

In a daze, she made her way towards where the men were working. Not looking where she was walking, she very nearly stumbled into a makeshift mass grave. Glancing down at one of the cadavers that had been rested on the edge of the pit, ready to be interred, she noticed something strange. This poor man was wearing the uniform they had clothed the prisoners in, he also had the blue tinges to his hair that denoted Azurian descendance. This man had not been killed in combat with a sword or a bow and arrow, he had been roughly impaled, similar to how many of the Rebels had been killed. 'They are killing their own now,' she muttered, more to herself than to anyone else. 'I have to get Alexander away from that witch.'

Once she had gotten over the horror of the situation, she knuckled down to help with the removal of the bodies and the cleaning of the remnants of battle.

It was dirty, disgusting, bloody, but solemn work.

When the last body had been buried in the pits, Bernard called his group together by the disguised hatchway to the tunnel. He wanted to brief them on what they were doing and how they should conduct their search. 'It's been a terrible morning for all of us. We don't know what lies in wait for us as we enter these tunnels. We do not know how to get word to Ambric that we're coming, or even how to find him.'

This last statement caused some consternation through his men.

'I know where he is,' Cassandra shouted from the back of the group.

The men turned, almost as one, to see who it was who had made the astonishing claim. Cassandra's face flushed with the attention. All eyes were on her, eager for her to tell them what she knew.

'I know where he is. I cannot go into detail of *how* I know, not yet anyway, but I'm asking you to trust me.' Her next statement would be a gamble, one that she knew she would have to explain later, but also one she knew she had to take. 'Your prince, Bernard, has faith in me. I ask the same from you. If you can trust me, I will lead us to our men, and we can continue our fight to free Carnelia from the tyranny of Azuria, and from the witch Endellion!'

Everyone looked to Bernard, including Cassandra.

He shot a glance to her; his face like thunder, but he smiled.

She smiled back.

'It's true, she does have my trust. Now, it will be slow going when we get inside. If I know Ambric, and I do, then the way will be paved with many traps and pitfalls. We must be vigilant. We'll break camp in one hour. May the Glimm guide us every step of the way.'

As the men got ready, Bernard opened the hatch and carefully stepped into the darkness below. He beckoned a worried looking Cassandra to follow him inside.

~~~~

'What are you playing at, Cass?' he spat. 'How do you know where Ambric is? Why did you just lie to the men about having my trust on this?'

Cassandra's head was bowed low. Her hand was on the Glimmer in her pocket. Although she couldn't see it, she knew it would be glowing, a deep blue throb.

'If I tell you, will you believe me?'

'Believe you? Right now, I want to throttle you. Why would you tell the men that you know where Ambric is?'

'Because I do.' Without another word she produced the glowing orb from her pocket.

Bernard's eyes were instantly drawn to the oddity. 'The Glimmer?' he asked.

'It has given me the power of remote seeing. I can see where their camp is.'

'With this glowing ball?'

Cassandra nodded.

'And this power is to be believed?'

She swallowed before answering. 'Yes, and no.'

Again, Bernard regarded her as if he had never laid eyes on her before.

'Yes, as in the power this orb holds is almost unlimited, but no, as in I do not know how to use it properly, yet.' Her pleading eyes never left his. They were begging for understanding. 'It's difficult to explain. But, using this Glimmer, I was able to find our way out of the woods that day. Remember?'

Bernard never reacted.

'It allows me to produce the butterflies.'

He nodded.

'I don't have anywhere near the ability that Endellion has, but my guides, they tell me I am a natural.'

'Guides?'

She nodded, not willing to go into any depth of the men and the throne room, they didn't have the time. 'I've seen Ambric, and his men. They're holed up within the tunnels. I know where they are. You need to trust me.'

Bernard breathed a deep sigh. 'You are asking me to put a lot of faith into this talisman. One you profess not to fully understand.'

Without even thinking about it, Cassandra leaned in and kissed him.

After the initial shock of the embrace, he held her and kissed her back. 'Are you trying to seduce me, Queen Cassandra?' he asked. There was humour in his voice.

She shook her head.

'I'm not *trying* anything,' she replied.

5.

FROM BEHIND A bush, not far from the makeshift camp, and now the makeshift mass grave, a face appeared. The face belonged to a man. His hair was tinged blue, and he was wearing the armour of an Azurian Knight. 'They have entered the tunnels,' he whispered to someone unseen behind him. 'Let's give them an hour so they believe they are alone in there. Then we follow.'

'An hour? They could be anywhere by then. We need to go in now.'

The man grinned. 'No, they won't. I overheard them talking about traps and pitfalls. They'll be leaving a trail behind them that a five-year-old could follow. Let the queen know we'll be moving in an hour.'

'Yes, sir.' The unseen man made his way back through the bush. After a short distance, he came to a clearing. Inside the clearing was an army of fireflies, lined up and waiting patiently for their orders from their queen.

6.

THE JOURNEY THROUGH the tunnels was slow. As predicted, Ambric had indeed booby-trapped their trail. He had improvised with sharpened tree roots and vines. He had set up precarious land falls that, if caught in them, would have trapped pursuers underground for days.

Due to Ambric's ingenuity, every few meters of tunnel had to be checked carefully, otherwise they were likely to lose men.

Eventually, they came across a fork in the tunnel, and the entourage came to a halt.

Bernard was busy analysing the entrances to both tunnels.

One of the men indicated a loose patch of earth in the right-hand tunnel. It looked like it had been recently disturbed. Bernard passed his torch to the soldier next to him and pressed a lose vine into the patch. When he laid on pressure, a series of sharpened sticks from below and from the sides sprung at them.

'Sir,' the man who found the trap spoke up. 'I believe he went into this tunnel. It makes sense if that's the one he booby-trapped.'

As the men readied themselves to enter the right-hand tunnel, Bernard was still regarding both entrances. He shook his head and grinned. 'You wily old bastard,' he muttered to himself. 'Wait ...' he shouted. This time he was talking to his party. 'It's a bluff. He's gone down the left-hand tunnel.'

Everyone looked at him. 'Are you sure?' the soldier asked. 'Why would he go through the bother of booby-trapping the wrong tunnel?'

'To throw any pursuer who had gotten through the first set of booby-traps off his scent. You know yourself how resourceful he is. Men ...' he addressed the rest of the party. 'We take the left tunnel!'

'Are you sure about this?' Cassandra whispered as everyone prepared to enter. She didn't want to undermine his leadership by asking him outright.

He nodded his reply, flashing her a smile. It was reassurance enough for her.

The going was even slower after that. The men set off methodically testing for booby-traps along the way but found few. It seemed that Ambric had assumed the pursuers would have fallen for his tricks, and he would have wanted to put a fair bit of distance between himself and them.

The group traversed the underground terrain for many hours before deciding to make a camp for the night. It was deemed tents were not required, as they were under cover anyways, but they would need a couple of small fires. They needed to be small so as not to burn up the oxygen within the tunnels and not to smoke the entourage to death. The area they had chosen looked, to Bernard, to have been used as a camp before. Although well-hidden, the evidence was there of ashes and roughly buried graves for chickens and squirrels. He knew if they had used this location, then there must have been ample ventilation to allow for the fires.

That night, they rested, and it was uneventful.

The next morning, they were up early, a makeshift breakfast was prepared, and they were back marching within an hour. As they were less concerned about booby-traps, they covered quite a bit of ground.

'What are these tunnels for?' Cassandra asked as they walked.

'They're ancient. They go back to the original feuds between our two kingdoms. During the wars, all trade routes were closed and heavily guarded. Nothing was allowed to be legally passed between the kingdoms. Everyone knows what happens when somebody tells somebody else, they're not allowed to do something. If they're determined enough...' Bernard raised his eyebrows for her. '...they'll find a way. So, these tunnels were mined. It's said they were dug by collaborative teams from both kingdoms, working together for a common cause. Some historians have theorised that it could have been one of the reasons for the original truce to be formed. Even though I've never personally been in them, Ambric used them for years for training purposes. If anyone alive knows these tunnels better then Ambric, I'd be surprised.'

7.

FOLLOWING BEHIND AT a safe distance, one that was enough to not be heard or tracked, was a contingency of Azurian soldiers. These men were accompanied by several monstrous fireflies. The insects had been commanded to crawl while in the tunnels as the beating of their wings would have given them away, jeopardising the element of surprise when the time came to attack.

The men were wary of the beasts but had been told they were to trust them as they were loyal to the queen. Not one man questioned how the queen had come about the skills to command these abhorrent insects; they were too focused on the job at hand.

Endellion had not entered the tunnels. She and Alexander, and another contingent of guards, had camped outside the hatch. They would wait where the Ferals had camped prior to entering. Their job was to slaughter any, and all, who tried to escape the oncoming attack.

She spent most of the time in her tent, alone, leaving orders to not be disturbed by anyone, even Alexander. The use of the Glimmer did not court company, or witnesses. The red glow coming from her tent worried Alexander, but he had his orders, and he intended to keep them to the best of his abilities.

Endellion was sitting in the centre of her tent, her legs crossed beneath her. The glowing Glimmer was cradled within her hands. She had initiated the ability of remote sight and was currently seeing everything happening in the tunnels through the eyes of the lead firefly. *Leopold, Halia, and Thaddius have all met my justice. Soon I'll have Ambric in my grasp. This time, he'll not escape,* she hissed in her head.

8.

AS THEY CONTINUED their march, Cassandra would occasionally drop back from the group or speed up ahead to consult her Glimmer, to activate her remote seeing ability. 'They're not far now,' she confided to Bernard after she had seen Ambric and his group eating around a fire. 'They've made camp.' She touched the Glimmer in her pocket again, only lightly. 'It's about five hundred yards around the next bend.' She indicated the way they were facing. 'Some of them are injured.'

'Has he posted any guards?' Bernard asked.

She briefly consulted her Glimmer again. 'Yes, but I know their exact locations.'

'Fantastic,' he said. 'Let's go and bring them back to safety.'

~~~~

'Ambric, are you there? Can you hear us?' Bernard shouted as they approached where Cassandra had reported the guards to be stationed.

As he, Cassandra, and another two of the vanguard made it around the bend in the tunnel, a guard wearing the armour of Carnelia held a long spike on a pole pointed towards them. His sword was sheathed at his side. Bernard noted that the arm not holding the spike was bandaged from the elbow up and there was a dark stain down the leg of his tunic.

'Who goes there?' the guard shouted. The way he held his head told Bernard he was shouting loud enough for another guard behind him to hear. He guessed more heavily armed men would be turning up in moments.

'It's me, Bernard of the Ferals. We've come to bring you back to Outpost Three.'

'Bernard, my prince. Thank the gods,' a voice from behind the guard shouted. Bernard recognised it and couldn't help breaking into a smile as Ambric appeared from the darkness. Never the one to dwell on niceties, especially when there was work to be done, Ambric's smile soon fell from his face. 'We have many injured, some badly. You have come at the right ti—LOOK OUT!'

Ambric's shout startled everyone.

Bernard turned, unsheathing his sword, as was his training. He was just in time to see one of his men being torn apart by the sting of an approaching firefly. It had been crawling towards them but had twisted its body to use its sting as a weapon. With revulsion rising in his stomach,

274

Bernard watched as the beast swung its thorax from left to right, slicing its lethal barb through the man's body, effortlessly tearing him in half.

Another firefly rushed towards two more of his men. They had time to turn and strike at the beast before its wicked, dripping sting found purchase. As the beast fell, dying, another three rushed out of the darkness.

'Bernard, to me. Quickly,' Ambric shouted as he spied movement behind the oncoming beasts. Bernard turned to see where his mentor was looking. He felt his flesh crawl; the darkness itself was moving, creeping and crawling over itself.

The swarm of fireflies burst into the light of the flickering torches. They took another three men, far too easily for Bernard's liking. Wet ripping noises filled his ears. Stabbing, tearing and screaming could be heard from behind them as Bernard took Cassandra's arm, dragging her towards Ambric and the relative safety of the compound.

Ambric was charging forward, as were several of his men. They ran at the fireflies, intending to engage them within the tight quarters of the tunnel. As he charged past Bernard and Cassandra, he took one look at them and stopped dead in his tracks. 'Cassandra …' he hissed.

She looked at him. She could see distrust in his eyes and his hand on the hilt of his sword.

'Bernard, why have you brought her here? It could be her who is controlling these beasts. We have no way of knowing. You may have led the enemy to our door.'

As the words left his mouth, he turned quickly to ward off an attack. In one fluid movement, his sword was unsheathed, and the enemy's sting lay on the floor, covered in yellow, viscous liquid. Without looking back at the couple, he was off, taking the fight to the approaching hoard.

'What did he mean, bringing the enemy to the door?' Cassandra asked.

Bernard was looking confused towards Ambric, who was now engaging two fireflies in open combat. 'Stay here,' he ordered. 'And stay safe. Find somewhere to hide. Don't go inside the compound until I find out what Ambric meant.'

As Bernard charged off to fight next to Ambric, Cassandra found a small nook in the wall of the tunnel and climbed inside. She watched as the bloody battle commenced around her. The men in their riding party, all that were left of them, were vehemently fighting off beasts. She longed to join them, to help, but she had made a promise to Bernard to stay safe.

'Don't go for the heads …' Ambric shouted from the frontline of their defence. 'Go for their stings. If they lose them, they wither and die!'

Cassandra watched as the expert swordsman cut open and killed another two of the horrific monsters.

9

THE BATTLE WAS bloody. Torn limbs, both insect and human, littered the floor of the tunnel. Pools of dark red and glowing yellow gathered in the uneven surfaces of the compacted earth and spattered over the walls and ceiling. Since the Azurian men had joined the battle, both sides were taking heavy casualties.

It was exactly what Endellion wanted.

As she watched through the eyes of her fireflies, flicking from one to another as many of them were slaughtered and fell, she watched Ambric battling bravely, cutting a swathe through her horde of insects. Her eyes were closed as she gripped the Glimmer tighter, working hard, coordinating the battle. 'Capture Ambric, but do not kill him. I want him brought back. He needs to answer for his crimes against me.' She sent this message telepathically to her fireflies.

Suddenly, she could see Ambric inundated with attacking insects. They swarmed over him, smothering him. However, he steadfastly

277

refused to give in. He hacked away, cutting and slicing his enemy, showing no sign of tiring. Two insects charged him, knocking him off his feet, then another two pinned him down. Before he knew what was happening, there were four, then five. Each using their insectoid legs to hold him. It was proving difficult as he stubbornly refused to yield. He cut at their legs, wings, and bodies, but they kept on coming.

One firefly took to the air and charged down at him. It took hold of his body by the shoulders and lifted him off the ground. Another appeared and grabbed his thrashing legs, then another grappled the sword from his hands.

Endellion was delighted with what she was seeing.

'There is that sappy prince. The son of Thaddius and the weak-minded bitch he married,' she hissed. 'Do I kill him? Or do I allow him to watch as I take their leader and slowly hunt down, and kill, the rest of their stupid Ferals and Rebels?' Her musings were amusing her until she spied something.

She could not believe her luck.

10.

AMBRIC WAS SCREAMING. He was not in pain, his screams were in defiance of the insects that held him, taking him prisoner. It had long been said that when the day came for Robert Ambric to die, he would not go out without a damned good fight.

Bernard battled his way through to where the fireflies were hovering, holding his mentor captive. His sword slashed at them, but to his dismay, they were just out of his reach. He turned his sweat- and blood-gritted face towards Cassandra, who was hiding in a nook in the wall. 'Cass, get yourself into the compound now. If I can, I'll join you shortly.'

Bernard focused his attentions back onto the fireflies as he heard her exit the nook and head to safety. She was holding the Glimmer in her hands. She had been trying to use it to counter something against the fireflies. Hoping beyond hope that maybe her butterflies could do a job. She had only been able to conjure twelve small sickly, creatures. The fireflies did not even notice they were there.

On Bernard's instruction to leave, she took the opportunity to run. She didn't notice one of the fireflies whip around to witness her exit. Watching and reporting it back to its queen. The creature ceased fighting and flew towards her. The fireflies who were holding Ambric looked in the same direction. Something about her interested them, like they were receiving unseen orders, and their interest in Ambric waned just for a moment. They dropped him, unceremoniously onto the bloody floor of the tunnel and, as one, flew to join their companion buzzing around Cassandra.

As Ambric hit the floor, he rolled, allowing himself to recover quickly. He looked up from his low vantage point and watched five of the insects surround the young queen and pick her up off the ground.

Her screams were pitiful. They were screams mirrored Ambric's own, only moments ago, they were screams of defiance, but also fear, as she struggled against her overwhelming captors. The fireflies raised her from the ground just as Bernard rushed at them.

Ambric could see the mistake in his charge instantly.

He was rash, not thinking. His sword was raised high, pointing towards his enemy.

'Bernard, protect your body,' he shouted. 'Protect your body, boy!'

Everything that happened next was in slow motion.

A firefliy saw Bernard's charge from afar.

The boy had overreached his attack, and the monster parried the charge, easily dodging the raised sword. Ambric saw the insect raised its thorax, exposing its huge, dangerous sting.

He recovered quickly from his overswing, but the firefly raised its sting catching Bernard in his chest. The slow arc of its thorax tore through the boy's clothes and skin. The spray of blood covered the insect as the boy's body fell limp.

The insect lowered its body, and Bernard's ruined torso slipped from the sting, falling to the floor. His sword fell from his wilting hand and his head turned. With only a surprised expression, his vacant, pink eyes looked towards Cassandra.

'Noooooo …' she screamed. 'Bernard, no!'

The fireflies holding her raised her higher, preparing to escape from what remained of the battle, off in the direction from which they came.

'Ambric! Ambric. Bernard. Help him,' she screamed at the former knight, who was now kneeling at Bernard's side.

~~~~~

He turned towards the queen hovering above him. The hatred for what he thought she might be and what she might have done to his group, his friend, and his prince, was etched into his fierce eyes.

As this exchanged happened, the remaining fireflies broke from the battle and joined Cass's captors in the air.

At the same time, what was left of the Azurian soldiers also broke and began their retreat. They backed off, down the tunnels, illuminated by the glow from the fireflies.

Ambric watched with a heavy heart as the beasts holding Cassandra hovered above him. 'Why do you want me to help him? You brought this upon us! You have brought death twice to me now, Queen Cassandra. The next time I see you, it will be you and your servant, the witch Endellion, lying in blood. ON THIS I SWEAR!' Ambric shouted the last four words.

~~~~~

Cass didn't want to believe what she had just heard. Ambric was an ally, a fantastic ally, she hated the thought of him thinking she had betrayed them. Betrayed Carnelia. Betrayed Bernard.

Endellion, she thought, *it's Endellion, disguised as me. It's not me ...*

With this thought ringing in her head, she relaxed into the grip of the insects, excepting her fate.

'Anthony,' she called out as the beasts retreated down the tunnel, away from the battle, away from her fallen love.

She saw Ambric's head cock to one side, and she hoped he had heard her. It was her code word, the word chosen for the men to understand who she was.

A tear slipped down the side of her face. It hung from her cheek and another joined it. As they conjoined, they became heavy, and dripped from her chin.

'Bernard,' she whispered. 'Goodbye, my love.'

The City of the Fireflies

As the fireflies took her away, she was just able to wriggle her hand free enough to reach inside her secret pocket. Her fingertips found what they were searching for, and they caressed the cool surface of her Glimmer.

She closed her eyes.

11.

ENDELLION WATCHED THE progress of her army through the eyes of the leading insect as they flew back through the tunnels. It felt strange to feel happy again; it was almost an alien concept to her. She thought she had never been truly happy since the morning of the worst day of her life.

She remembered the gentle touch of her prince as they made love that final time, before her world changed.

Forever!

Right now, everything she'd wished for since that day, for the whole of her pathetic existence, would be hers.

~~~~

Ambric and what remained of the Ferals, and Rebels dragged the bodies of their dead and wounded into the compound. He was the last man to enter, and he slowly closed the hatch behind him. Shutting off the horrors of the battle that had raged briefly but bloodily beyond.

When they were inside, he ordered the wounded to be separated from the dead and for them to be tended. He selected a few of the remaining able-bodied men and set them an honourable task.

They were to dig graves for their fallen comrades.

Later that night, dog tired and covered in dried blood and dirt, Ambric sat as a lone guard at the doorway to their chambers. He put his head in his hands and wept.

12.

CASSANDRA WAS NO longer in the grip of the fireflies. She was stood in the dark throne room. Her Glimm guide was ever present and patiently waiting for her to speak. This time, however, his usual pleasant smile was not present. His facial features were solemn and grim.

'My guide,' Cass began. 'I have a favour to ask, and I do not have much time for it to be granted.'

Her guide smiled, and his face changed into something she was more accustomed to.

'Ask away, my child,' he grinned. 'We cannot deny you anything …'

Printed in Great Britain
by Amazon

84823781R00163